英汉对照典藏本

英国文艺复兴早期戏剧

浮士德博士的悲剧

[英] 克里斯托弗·马洛 著

陈才宇 译

Spirit

Air   Water

Earth   Fire

浙江工商大学出版社

· 杭州 ·

图书在版编目(CIP)数据

浮士德博士的悲剧/(英)克里斯托弗·马洛著；
陈才宇译. — 杭州：浙江工商大学出版社，2018.7
(2023.3 重印)
ISBN 978-7-5178-2814-3

Ⅰ.①浮… Ⅱ.①克… ②陈… Ⅲ.①长篇小说—英
国—现代 Ⅳ.①I561.45

中国版本图书馆 CIP 数据核字(2018)第 150455 号

浮士德博士的悲剧

[英]克里斯托弗·马洛 著 陈才宇 译

出 品 人	鲍观明	
策划编辑	钟仲南	
责任编辑	沈 娴	
责任校对	王黎明	
封面设计	观止堂_未氓	
责任印制	包建辉	
出版发行	浙江工商大学出版社	
	(杭州市教工路 198 号 邮政编码 310012)	
	(E-mail：zjgsupress@163.com)	
	(网址：http://www.zjgsupress.com)	
	电话：0571-88904980,88831806(传真)	
排 版	杭州朝曦图文设计有限公司	
印 刷	杭州宏雅印刷有限公司	
开 本	880mm×1230mm 1/32	
印 张	7.5	
字 数	174 千	
版 印 次	2018 年 7 月第 1 版 2023 年 3 月第 2 次印刷	
书 号	ISBN 978-7-5178-2814-3	
定 价	58.00 元	

译 序

　　《浮士德博士的悲剧》(*The Tragical History of Doctor Faustus*)是一部诗剧，作者是"大学才子"克里斯托弗·马洛(Christopher Marlowe,1564—1593)。

　　"大学才子"，是指英国文艺复兴初期具有大学教育背景的七位作家，即李雷、皮尔、劳契、格林、纳什、基德和马洛。他们的文学活动，尤其是戏剧创作，为莎士比亚准备了基础，因此又有"莎士比亚的先驱"之称。这几人中，成就最高的是马洛。

　　马洛出生于坎特伯雷一补鞋匠的家庭，就读于剑桥大学的圣体学院。他有才华，但也不安分：1589年，他参与一场街头斗殴，一位叫华森的诗人在斗殴中丧生。1592年，他因贩卖假币被荷兰政府驱逐出境。1593年，他在酒店与人争吵，赔上性命，年仅二十九岁。有人怀疑那是一场阴谋，即便是，阴谋者也是利用了他爱惹是生非的性格。

　　马洛写过多部戏剧，如《迦太基女王狄多的悲剧》(*Dido Queen of Carthage*)、《贴木儿大帝》(*Tamburlaine the Great*)、《马尔他的犹太人》(*The Jew of Malta*)、《爱德华二世》(*Edward II*)、《巴黎大屠杀》(*The Massacre at Paris*)等都是他的作品。他还翻译过奥维德的诗歌；创作过一首叙事诗《希罗与利安得》(*Hero and Leander*)，其中多有色情描写。一首题为《痴情的牧羊人致爱人》(*The Passionate Sherpherd to His Love*）的著名短诗，也是他写的。

《浮士德博士的悲剧》是马洛的戏剧代表作，写于1593年，即作者在世的最后一年。次年，由海军大臣剧团上演。书业公所登记在1603年。从艺术而言，这部诗剧也许不是他最成熟的一部，但影响巨大。学者们经常拿它与歌德的《浮士德》(*Faust*)做比较：相同的题材，两位诗人处理的手法不尽相同，可谓各有千秋。

浮士德是一个博学多才的术士，有关他的故事流传于16世纪的德国民间。1587年，法兰克福出版了一本记载他的传说的书*Faustbuch*，此书不久译成英文，书名译成《约翰·浮士德博士该诅咒的一生和天谴之死》(*The Historie of the Damnable Life，and Deserved Death of Doctor John Faustus*)。马洛利用这个英译本，但有所改造。在他的笔下，浮士德从一个魔术师蜕变为"巨人"的形象。他渴望得到无限的力量，甚至想主宰世界。为了满足自己的欲望，浮士德利用魔术招来魔鬼靡非斯特，与他签订一份契约：魔鬼为他服务二十四年，在此期间，必须听命于他，做他所要求的任何事。期满以后，魔鬼可以取走他的灵魂。在而后的场景中，契约得到了确实的履行。为了满足浮士德的情欲，魔鬼还为他招来古希腊的美女海伦。在魔鬼的帮助下，浮士德的欲望固然满足了，但随着契约期限的临近，他又陷入深深的苦恼中。但此时的浮士德已经万劫不复，只能任凭魔鬼摆布，坠入死亡的深渊。

马洛笔下的浮士德在关键点上与歌德的浮士德分道扬镳：马洛的浮士德是一个利己主义者，他的所作所为都为满足一己的私欲。等待他的结局只能是下地狱。歌德的浮士德具有博爱的精神，他将魔鬼为他掘墓的铁锹声误当作造福人类的劳动之声，并为此感到满足，喊出:"你真美呀,请停一下!"上帝最后派出天使,将他带上天堂。

《浮士德博士的悲剧》流传下来有A和B两个版本。A本是1604年出版的四开本,而后1609年和1611年又先后再版过。A本显然不是善本:作为文艺复兴时期的戏剧,篇幅就嫌短了些(译成汉语,仅4万字左右)。全剧十四场,不分幕。有关喜剧场景的文字也很草率,个别地方还有错置的现象。有人据此认为A本不是作者的原创本,而是演员凭记忆重构的本子。但近代学者倾向于另一种说法:A本应该是一个权威的"坏本",因为剧中的核心场景是可信的,属于马洛的创作无疑。

B本也是四开本,出版于1616年。1619—1663年间,共再版了六次。A本中有三十六行为B本所缺,但属于新增的部分却有六百七十六行之多。A本中字面的差错和脱漏,B本都一一加以更正,从而加强了可读性。有人统计过,光字面上的订正,就达上千处。全剧还分成五幕,格局符合文艺复兴时期的戏剧规范。在情节上,A本中有其言而无其行的几处,B本都进行了扩充。比如,有关超自然的场景,有关伪教皇的描写,B本都丰满起来了。全剧的结尾则加强了恐怖的效果:A本中由魔鬼上场,将浮士德带走,接着便是解说员的收场词。B本则是让魔鬼当着三位学者的面,肢解了浮士德的尸体!

A本和B本,究竟哪个版本更接近作者的原创?似乎依然是A本。但我仍坚持用B本来翻译这个剧。理由是:B本文字上的脱漏比A本少。B本的情节更丰满。A本中最精彩的部分,即肯定属于马洛手笔的一部分,B本都保留着。B本所增加的部分即便是后人添加,也属于合理化的扩充。

此外,还有更重要的一个原因:A本在我国已经有一个译本。1956

年,作家出版社出版了戴镏龄先生翻译的《浮士德博士的悲剧》,他依据的就是A本。我现在将B本译出,对普通读者增添了阅读的选择,对研究者则增加了研究的资料。

译得不地道处,切盼读者指教。

陈才宇

2018年4月25日于杭州寓所

CONTENTS/目录

剧中人物

The Chorus
解说员

Doctor John Faustus
约翰·浮士德博士

Wagner
瓦格纳

Good Angel
好天使

Bad Angel
坏天使

Valdes
瓦尔德斯

Cornelius
康奈琉斯

Three Scholars
三学者

Lucifer
魔王撒旦

Devils
魔鬼

Mephistopheles
靡非斯特

Robin, *the Clown*
罗宾　小丑

A Woman Devil
一女魔

Dick
狄克

Beelzebub
别西卜

Pride 骄傲		The Cardinal of France 法兰西红衣主教
Covetousness 贪婪		The Cardinal of Padua 帕多瓦红衣主教
Envy 妒忌		The Archbishop of Rheims 兰斯大主教
Wrath 愤怒	*The Seven Deadly Sins* 七大罪恶	The Bishop of Lorraine 洛林主教
Gluttony 饕餮		Monks 僧侣
Sloth 懒惰		Friars 修道士
Lechery 淫荡		A Vintner 酒店老板
Pope Adrian 教皇阿德里安		Martino 马丁诺
Raymond, King of Hungary 雷蒙德　匈牙利皇帝		Frederick 弗雷德里克
Bruno, *the rival pope* 布鲁诺　敌对的教皇		Officers 官员

3

Gentlemen
乡绅

Benvolio
班佛里奥

The Emperor of Germany, Charles V
查理五世 德国皇帝

The Duck of Saxony
萨克森公爵

Alexander the Great
亚历山大大帝

} Spirits
精灵

His Paramour
亚历山大大帝的情妇

Darius
大流士

Belimoth
贝利摩斯

Argiron
阿格隆

} Devils
魔鬼

Ashtaroth
艾希塔勒斯

Soldiers
士兵

A Horse-Courser
马贩

A Carter
马车夫

A Hostess
女店主

The Duck of Vanholt
凡豪特公爵

The Duchess of Vanholt
凡豪特公爵夫人

A Servant
一仆人

Helen of Troy, *a spirit*
特洛伊的海伦　一精灵

An Old Man
一老者

Two Cupids
两爱神

By Harry Clarke

哈里·克拉克 绘

PROLOGUE

序 幕

Enter Chorus

CHORUS   Not marching now in fields of Thrasimene,

Where Mars did mate the Carthaginians,

Nor sporting in the dalliance of love

In courts of kings where state is overturned,

Nor in the pomp of proud audacious deeds,

Intends our muse to vaunt her heavenly verse.

Only this, gentlemen: we must perform

The form of Faustus' fortunes, good or bad.

And now to patient judgments we appeal,

And speak for Faustus in his infancy.

Now is he born, his parents base of stock,

In Germany, within a town called Rhode.

At riper years to Wittenberg he went,

Whereas his kinsmen chiefly brought him up.

So much he profits in divinity

That shortly he was graced with doctor's name,

Excelling all, and sweetly can dispute

In th'heavenly matters of theology;

4

解说员上

解说员　这里没有大军奔赴特拉西梅诺[1]，

玛尔斯[2]曾在那里会盟迦太基人；

这里也没有宫廷的调情卖俏，

那是帝王之所好，亡国的征兆。

我们的缪斯[3]谱写美妙诗章，

从不渲染强横者创建的辉煌。

诸位看客，今天我们要开演

浮士德的一生，包括红运厄运。

请大家耐心旁观，做出评判。

我们首先要说他的孩提时代：

他出生在德国，家世寒微，

生养他的地方叫作罗得镇。

待到年岁稍长，他去了维腾堡，

他的生计主要靠亲友的周济。

由于在神学方面造诣颇深，

不久超越同道，获博士美名。

他善辩，尽管神学莫测高深，

他却说得头头是道，透彻而动人。

5

Till swoll'n with cunning of a self-conceit,

His waxen wings did mount above his reach,

And, melting, heavens conspired his overthrow.

For, falling to a devilish exercise,

And glutted now with learning's golden gifts,

He surfeits upon cursed necromancy;

Nothing so sweet as magic is to him,

Which he prefers before his chiefest bliss:

And this the man that in his study sits.

    [*Exit*]

直到他因此而得意,自命不凡,
总想凭蜡翼飞上不可及的天堂,
结果蜡翼融化,上天将他惩罚。
这只能怪他陷入魔鬼的圈套,
餍足了知识的金色馈赠,
便沉溺该诅咒的左道旁门;
他觉得万般唯魔术最可爱,
于是迷恋此道,忘了神的赐福。
这人眼下就坐在自己的书斋里。

[解说员下]

ACT 1

第一幕

SCENE 1

Faustus in his study

FAUSTUS   Settle thy studies, Faustus, and begin

To sound the depth of that thou wilt profess.

Having commenced, be a divine in show,

Yet level at the end of every art,

And live and die in Aristotle's works.

Sweet *Analytics*, 'tis thou hast ravished me!

[*He reads*] '*Bene disserere est finis logices.*'

Is, to dispute well, logic's chiefest end?

Affords this art no greater miracle?

Then read no more; thou hast attained that end.

A greater subject fitteth Faustus' wit.

Bid *Oeconomy* farewell, and Galen, come!

Be a physician, Faustus. Heap up gold,

And be eternized for some wondrous cure.

[*He reads*] '*Summum bonum medicinae sanitas*':

The end of physic is our body's health.

Why Faustus, hast thou not attained that end?

Are not thy bills hung up as monuments,

第一场

浮士德在书斋

浮士德　确定你的课业,浮士德,然后

对所选科目做穷源溯流的研究。

既然学位已得,且做个神学家,

同时钻研其他学科的微言奥义,

与亚里士多德的著作生死相依。

可爱的逻辑分析,你让我着迷!

[读]"逻辑学的最终目的在于辩论",

能言善辩,难道这就是逻辑学廉价的目标? [4]

难道它不创造更伟大的奇迹?

别读了,这一目的你已经达到。

浮士德的智慧适宜更高深的学问。

再见吧,经济学! 来吧,盖仑[5]。

做个医生吧,浮士德。日纳斗金,

创造医疗奇迹,永远名垂史册。

[读]"医学的目的在于治病救人":

医学的目的在于我们身体的健康。

浮士德,你不是如愿以偿了吗?

你开的药方成了张贴的纪念碑,

Whereby whole cities have escaped the plague,

And thousand desperate maladies been eased?

Yet art thou still but Faustus, and a man.

Couldst thou make men to live eternally,

Or, being dead, raise them to life again,

Then this profession were to be esteemed.

Physic, farewell! Where is Justinian?

[*He reads*] '*Si una eademque res legatur duobus*,

alter rem, alter valorem rei' , etc.

A petty case of paltry legacies!

[*He reads*] '*Exhoereditare filium non potest pater, nisi—*'

Such is the subject of the Institute,

And universal body of the law.

This study fits a mercenary drudge,

Who aims at nothing but external trash—

Too servile and illiberal for me.

When all is done, divinity is best.

Jerome's Bible, Faustus; view it well.

[*He reads*] '*Stipendium peccati mors est.*' Ha!

'*Stipendium*' , etc.

The reward of sin is death? That's hard.

[*He reads*] '*Si peccasse negamus, fallimur*

Et nulla est in nobis veritas.'

If we say that we have no sin,

we deceive ourselves, and there's no truth in us.

多少城市依靠它们躲过了瘟疫，
数以千计的恶疾凭它们得到治疗。
只是你依然是浮士德，一介凡人。
如果你能让人永生不死，
或者让一个已死的人重获生命，
那时医学这行当才值得尊敬。
再见吧，医学！《民法大全》[6]何在？
[读]"倘若某一物品由两人继承，一人
得其物，另一人得相当价值之货币。"
一条微不足道的继承法条文！
[读]"父亲不能剥夺儿子的继承权，除非——"
这是法典里讨论的一个题目，
值得普天下执法机构的关注。
但这样的研究只适合贪财的苦工，
因为他只为身外的废物而活——
对于我，这太低俗，也太浮浅了。
权衡之下，最有用的还是神学。
浮士德，细读杰罗姆的《圣经》吧。
[读]"罪的工价乃是死，"[7]哈！
"工价"——
罪的代价是死亡？太严酷了。
[读]"我们若说自己无罪，便是
自欺，真理不在我们心里了。"[8]
我们若言自身无原罪，
就是自欺，我们心中没有真理。

13

Why then belike we must sin,

and so consequently die.

Ay, we must die an everlasting death.

What doctrine call you this? *Che serà, serà:*

What will be, shall be? Divinity, adieu

    [He picks up a book of magic]

These metaphysics of magicians

And necromantic books are heavenly,

Lines, circles, scenes, letters, and characters—

Ay, these are those that Faustus most desires.

O, what a world of profit and delight,

Of power, of honour, of omnipotence,

Is promised to the studious artizan!

All things that move between the quiet poles

Shall be at my command. Emperors and kings

Are but obeyed in their several provinces,

But his dominion that exceeds in this,

Stretcheth as far as doth the mind of man.

A sound magician is a demigod.

Here tire thy brains to gain a deity.

Wagner!

    Enter Wagner

    Commend me to my dearest friends,

The German Valdes and Cornelius.

Request them earnestly to visit me.

嘻,这么说,我们必然犯罪,

结果也就不免一死。哎呀,

我们必然死亡,归于永恒之死。

这又算什么教义?"凡存在的,

就一定存在。"再见吧,神学!

　　　　[他捡起一本魔法书]

魔法师的这些秘术玄言,

有关巫道的书,这才是绝学,

线条、圆圈、字母、符号——

这些玩意才合浮士德的心意。

哦,这是怎样一个追名逐利、

争权寻欢、无所不能的世界啊!

这世界属于勤奋的手艺人!

两极间一切活动着的生物

都得听我的召唤!所有的帝王

只能在各自的领地发号施令,

唯魔法师的权势超越国界,

直抵人的想象力所及的极限。

优秀的魔法师就是半个神仙!

我要费点神,先弄个神的名分。

瓦格纳!

　　瓦格纳上

　　你给我去见两个德国人,

我的朋友瓦尔德斯和康奈琉斯,

请他们马上到我这里来一趟。

WAGNER   I will, sir.

Exit [*Wagner*]

FAUSTUS   Their conference will be a greater help to me

Than all my labours, plod I ne'er so fast.

Enter the [*Good*] *Angel and Spirit* [*i.e. the Bad Angel*]

GOOD ANGEL   O, Faustus, lay that damned book aside

And gaze not on it, lest it tempt thy soul

And heap God's heavy wrath upon thy head!

Read, read the Scriptures. That is blasphemy.

BAD ANGEL   Go forward, Faustus, in that famous art

Wherein all nature's treasure is contained.

Be thou on earth as Jove is in the sky,

Lord and commander of these elements.

Exeunt Angels

FAUSTUS   How am I glutted with conceit of this!

Shall I make spirits fetch me what I please?

Resolve me of all ambiguities?

Perform what desperate enterprise I will?

I'll have them fly to India for gold,

Ransack the ocean for orient pearl,

And search all corners of the new-found world

For pleasant fruits and princely delicates.

I'll have them read me strange philosophy

And tell the secrets of all foreign kings.

I'll have them wall all Germany with brass

瓦格纳　是,先生。

　　　　[瓦格纳]下

浮士德　跟他们说说话对我有好处,

　　　　一个人苦苦钻研,实在太烦闷。

　　　　　　[好]天使与幽灵[即坏天使]上

好天使　浮士德哟,放下那该死的书吧,

　　　　别读它了,免得它诱惑你的灵魂,

　　　　从而使上帝将怒火发泄到你身上。

　　　　要读就读《圣经》。别亵渎神明了。

坏天使　继续读下去,浮士德,自然的瑰宝

　　　　全隐藏在这门绝妙的艺术中。

　　　　掌握这些元素,做它们的主人,

　　　　那时地上的你就是天上的神。

　　　　　　两天使下

浮士德　我豪饮的是怎样的奇思妙想啊!

　　　　我要不要让精灵为我奔走?

　　　　该不该让他们为我排忧解难?

　　　　为我开创梦寐以求的冒险事业?

　　　　我要派他们飞往印度采金,

　　　　到海底为我搜寻晶莹的珍珠,

　　　　到新大陆去,踏遍海角天涯,

　　　　搜集各种仙果和山珍海味。

　　　　我要让他们为我诵读海外奇文,

　　　　向我通报异域君主的深宫秘事。

　　　　我要让他们给德国筑起一道铜墙,

And make swift Rhine circle fair Wittenberg.

I'll have them fill the public schools with silk,

Wherewith the students shall be bravely clad.

I'll levy soldiers with the coin they bring,

And chase the Prince of Parma from our land,

And reign sole king of all the provinces;

Yea, stranger engines for the brunt of war,

Than was the fiery keel at Antwerp bridge,

I'll make my servile spirits to invent.

Come, German Valdes and Cornelius,

And make me blest with your sage conference!

Enter Valdes and Cornelius

Valdes, sweet Valdes, and Cornelius,

Know that your words have won me at the last

To practice magic and concealed arts.

Philosophy is odious and obscure;

Both law and physic are for petty wits,

'Tis magic, magic, that hath ravished me.

Then, gentle friends, aid me in this attempt,

And I, that have with concise syllogisms

Gravelled the pastors of the German Church,

And made the flow'ring pride of Wittenberg

Swarm to my problems as th' infernal spirits

On sweet Musaeus when he came to hell,

Will be as cunning as Agrippa was,

让莱茵河绕着美丽的维腾堡奔流。
我要让他们在校园里堆满丝绸，
让所有的学生都穿戴得漂漂亮亮。[9]
我要用他们带来的钱财征兵，
将帕马[10]王子赶出我们的国土，
让自己登基，做万邦的君主。
对了，我还要命令为我服务的精灵
发明武器用于冲锋陷阵，其威力
远超炸毁安特卫普大桥的火船。[11]
来，德国的瓦尔德斯和康奈琉斯，
让我听听两位好友的高见。

　　瓦尔德斯和康奈琉斯上
亲爱的瓦尔德斯、康奈琉斯，
你们说过的话已经将我说服，
我决意试一试魔法和巫道。
哲学不仅令人讨厌，还晦涩难懂，
法律和医道只适宜耍小聪明的人。
魔法，只有魔法，能让我着迷。
两位好友，帮我试试魔法吧；
我曾经运用繁复的三段论法，
说得德国教会的牧师颜面扫地，
全维腾堡的雅士高人都赶来聆听
我的宏论，那情景就像穆赛俄斯[12]
在地狱用歌声吸引冥界的精灵。
现在我要像阿格里巴[13]那样显示神通，

Whose shadow made all Europe honour him.

VALDES   Faustus, these books, thy wit, and our experience

Shall make all nations to canonize us.

As Indian Moors obey their Spanish lords,

So shall the spirits of every element

Be always serviceable to us three.

Like lions shall they guard us when we please,

Like Almaine rutters with their horsemen's staves,

Or Lapland giants, trotting by our sides;

Sometimes like women, or unwedded maids,

Shadowing more beauty in their airy brows

Than has the white breasts of the Queen of Love.

From Venice shall they drag huge argosies,

And from America the golden fleece

That yearly stuffs old Philip's treasury,

If learned Faustus will be resolute.

FAUSTUS   Valdes, as resolute am I in this

As thou to live. Therefore object it not.

CORNELIUS   The miracles that magic will perform

Will make thee vow to study nothing else.

He that is grounded in astrology,

Enriched with tongues, well seen in minerals,

Hath all the principles magic doth require.

Then doubt not, Faustus, but to be renowned

And more frequented for this mystery

招来鬼魂,让全欧洲对他肃然起敬。

瓦尔德斯 浮士德,凭这魔法书、凭你的智慧

和我们的经验,普天下的人都得

向我们顶礼膜拜,一如印度的沼泽

臣服于西班牙主子,各元素的精灵

一定忠心耿耿服务我们三人。

只要我们愿意,他们就是护卫的狮子,

就是手提长矛的日耳曼骑士,

或者是为我们奔走的拉普兰巨人。

有时精灵就像女人,或未婚的少女,

她们清秀的眉宇间投射出的美

胜过爱情女王那一对雪白的双乳。

只要饱学的浮士德拿定主意,

她们能从威尼斯拖来商船,

能从老腓力普王充裕的金库

取来产自美洲大陆的金羊毛。

浮士德 瓦尔德斯,我的主意确定无虚,

就像你的生命。好,这没有疑义。

康奈琉斯 魔法固然能创造种种奇迹,

但你得保证不再研习其他学问。

一个人只要以星相学为基础,

精通语言,并掌握炼丹术,

就拥有了魔法所需的根本。

别犹豫,浮士德,等着扬名吧,

为这法术,天下人都会知道你的名字,

Than heretofore the Delphian oracle.

The spirits tell me they can dry the sea

And fetch the treasure of all foreign wrecks—

Yea, all the wealth that our forefathers hid

Within the massy entrails of the earth

Then tell me, Faustus, what shall we three want?

FAUSTUS   Nothing, Cornelius. O, this cheers my soul!

Come, show me some demonstrations magical,

That I may conjure in some bushy grove

And have these joys in full possession.

VALDES   Then haste thee to some solitary grove,

And bear wise Bacon's and Albertus' works,

The Hebrew Psalter, and New Testament;

And whatsoever else is requisite

We will inform thee ere our conference cease.

CORNELIUS   Valdes, first let him know the words of art,

And then, all other ceremonies learned,

Faustus may try his cunning by himself.

VALDES   First I'll instruct thee in the rudiments,

And then wilt thou be perfecter than I.

FAUSTUS   Then come and dine with me, and after meat,

We'll canvass every quiddity thereof,

For ere I sleep I'll try what I can do.

This night I'll conjure, though I die therefore.

Exeunt

你的声音将胜过阿波罗的神谕。

精灵对我说过:他们能叫海水干枯,

能从外国的沉船里将财宝捞起——

是的,我们祖先的宝藏,哪怕藏于

结实的地心,他们都能为你取来。

浮士德,告诉我,我们还缺什么?

浮士德 不缺了,康奈琉斯,你说得中听!

来吧,先为我示范一下魔法,

待会我自个儿到林子里念咒,

尽情享受魔法所缔造的快乐。

瓦尔德斯 快去吧,找个僻静的林子,

带上培根和阿尔伯特[14]的著作,

希伯来文的《诗篇》和《新约》。

除此之外还需准备什么,

过一会我们会告诉你。

康奈琉斯 瓦尔德斯,先传授他口诀吧,

然后再让他学习各种仪式,

再以后他就可以自己一试身手了。

瓦尔德斯 让我先教会你一些基本法则,

往后你必定青出于蓝胜于蓝。

浮士德 来,我们先吃饭,吃完饭后,

再来逐一探讨魔法的本质。

睡觉以前,我定要试试身手,

即便因此而死,也要念上几段咒。

同下

SCENE 2

Enter two Scholars

FIRST SCHOLAR   I wonder what's become of Faustus, that was wont to make our schools ring with '*sic probo*'.

Enter Wagner, [carrying wine]

SECOND SCHOLAR   That shall we presently know, for see, here comes his boy.

FIRST SCHOLAR   How now, sirrah! Where's thy master?

WAGNER   God in heaven knows.

SECOND SCHOLAR   Why, dost not thou know, then?

WAGNER   Yes, I know, but that follows not.

FIRST SCHOLAR   Go to, sirrah! Leave your jesting, and tell us where he is.

WAGNER   That follows not by force of argument, which you, being licentiates, should stand upon. Therefore, acknowledge your error, and be attentive.

SECOND SCHOLAR   Then you will not tell us?

WAGNER   You are deceived, for I will tell you. Yet if you were not dunces, you would never ask me such a question. For is not he *corpus naturale*? And is not that *mobile*? Then, wherefore should you ask me such a question? But that I am by nature phlegmatic, slow to wrath, and prone to lechery—to love, I would say—it were

24

第二场

二学者上

学者甲　浮士德在我们学校,老是嚷嚷"由此我证明",不知这家伙现在怎么样了。

学者乙　过一会就知道了。看,他的弟子来了。

瓦格纳[携酒]上

学者甲　喂,先生,你的主人哪里去了?

瓦格纳　天知道。

学者乙　怎么,你不知道吗?

瓦格纳　不,我知道的。你们的推理错了[15]。

学者甲　得了吧,先生!别开玩笑了,告诉我们:他在哪里?

瓦格纳　从逻辑推论,不能得出那样的结论,你俩是硕士,说话得讲究逻辑。好了,认个错,下次说话注意点。

学者乙　你是不想告诉我们了?

瓦格纳　又推论错了,我会告诉你们的。如果你们不是傻瓜,就不会提这样的问题。浮士德不就是一个"自然物体"吗?凡自然物体就不免要"移动",是不是?你们为什么还要问我这样一个问题呢?要不是我天生是个冷淡的人,不会轻易发火,只是有点好色——应该

not for you to come within forty foot of the place of execution, although I do not doubt to see you both hanged the next sessions. Thus, having triumphed over you, I will set my countenance like a precisian, and begin to speak thus: Truly, my dear brethren, my master is within at dinner with Valdes and Cornelius, as this wine, if it could speak, would inform your worships. And so the Lord bless you, preserve you, and keep you, my dear brethren, my dear brethren.

    Exit [*Wagner*]

FIRST SCHOLAR   O Faustus,

    Then I fear that which I have long suspect,

    That thou art fall'n into that damned art

    for which they two are infamous through the world.

SECOND SCHOLAR   Were he a stranger, and not allied to me,

    The danger of his soul would make me mourn.

    But, come, let us go and inform the Rector.

    It may be his grave counsel may reclaim him.

FIRST SCHOLAR   I fear me nothing will reclaim him now.

SECOND SCHOLAR   Yet let us try what we can do.

    Exeunt

说有爱心——你们是不应该出现在这四十步的执行范围内的，尽管我并不怀疑下次开庭时就看见你们双双上绞架受死。我把你们打败了，现在应该摆出一副新教徒的神情，对你们说：不错，我的好兄弟，我的主人正在跟瓦尔德斯和康奈琉斯用膳。我手中这瓶酒，如果它能开口，也会这样向阁下通报。愿主赐福你们，保护你们，赡养你们，我的好兄弟。

　　[瓦格纳]下

学者甲　浮士德啊，

我一直都在担心

你已经迷上那该死的魔法；

那两人专于此道，早已远近闻名。

学者乙　即便他是个与我无关的陌生人，

他灵魂的堕落也让我痛心。

走，我们把事情报告校长去，

他的忠告也许能将他挽救。

学者甲　我担心现在没有任何事能让他回头。

学者乙　我们只能尽力而为了。

　　　　同下

SCENE 3

*Thunder. Enter Lucifer and four Devils [above]. [Enter] Faustus
to them with this speech. [He holds a book, unaware of their
presence]*

FAUSTUS   Now that the gloomy shadow of the night,

Longing to view Orion's drizzling look,

Leaps from th'Antarctic world unto the sky

And dims the welkin with her pitchy breath,

Faustus, begin thine incantations,

And try if devils will obey thy hest,

Seeing thou hast prayed and sacrificed to them.

[He draws a circle]

Within this circle is Jehovah's name,

Forward and backward anagrammatized,

Th'abbreviated names of holy saints,

Figures of every adjunct to the heavens,

And characters of signs and erring stars,

By which the spirits are enforced to rise.

Then fear not, Faustus, but be resolute,

And try the uttermost magic can perform.

第三场

雷声。魔王偕四魔鬼上[舞台上方];浮士德上,
口中念念有词。[他手握一本书,不知魔鬼的存
在]

浮士德 黑夜那幽暗阴沉的巨影
渴望一睹猎户星沾雨的面容,
正从南极边地跃入苍穹,
用乌黑的气息将天宇遮蔽,
浮士德,念起你的咒语吧!
你已做过祈祷,献过牺牲,
就该试试魔鬼是否恭敬从命。
　　[他在地上画了一个圈]
这圈子里有耶和华的名字,
字母被颠倒,词序被打乱,
此外还有缩写的圣徒名,
天上每一颗恒星的图形
以及十二宫和行星的标记,
凭此就能迫使精灵显身。
别害怕,浮士德,坚强些,
务必将魔法演示淋漓尽致。

29

Thunder

Sint mihi dei Acherontis propitii! Valeat numen triplex Jehovoe! Ignei, aerii, aquatici, terreni, spiritus, salvete! Orientis princeps Lucifer, Beelzebub, inferni ardentis monarcha, et Demogorgon, propitiamus vos, ut appareat et surgat Mephistopheles. Quod tu meraris? Per Jehovam, Gehennam, et consecratam aquam quam nunc spargo, signumque crucis quod nunc facio, et per vota nostra, ipse nunc surgat nobis dicatus Mephistopheles!

[*Faustus sprinkles holy water and makes a sign of the cross.*]

Enter a Devil [*Mephistopheles, in the shape of a*] *dragon*

I charge thee to return and change thy shape,

Thou art too ugly to attend on me.

Go, and return an old Franciscan friar;

That holy shape becomes a devil best.

Exit Devil [*Mephistopheles*]

I see there's virtue in my heavenly words.

Who would not be proficient in this art?

How pliant is this Mephistopheles,

Full of obedience and humility!

Such is the force of magic and my spells.

Enter Mephistopheles [*dressed as a friar*]

MEPHISTOPHELES Now, Faustus, what wouldst thou have me do?

FAUSTUS I charge thee wait upon me whilst I live,

To do whatever Faustus shall command,

Be it to make the moon drop from her sphere,

雷声又起

冥河的神灵啊,保佑我吉祥遂心! 愿三位一体的耶和华坚如磐石! 万福,火、气、水、土的精灵! 早晨之子[16]啊,你是东方的王子,别西卜,你是地狱中火牢的主宰,还有阴曹地府的魔王啊,我恳求你们让靡非斯特显身。为什么还要拖延?凭耶和华和地狱之名,凭我此刻洒下的圣水,凭我画出的十字架,凭我的祈祷,责令靡非斯特即刻显身!

[浮士德洒圣水,画十字。]

魔鬼[龙身的靡非斯特]上

我命令你回去换个相貌,

你这般丑陋,不配做我的跟班。

去吧,扮成芳济会的老修士,

那尊容最适宜魔鬼装扮。

魔鬼[靡非斯特]下

看来我这神咒倒真管用:

这门法术何人不想精通?

靡非斯特又是何等温顺,

他真够听话,真够谦逊!

这就是魔法和咒语的力量。

靡非斯特[扮修士]上

靡非斯特　浮士德,现在您有什么吩咐?

浮士德　我命令你服侍我的一生,

浮士德要你干啥,你就干啥,

不管是要月亮从天上掉下,

Or the ocean to overwhelm the world.

MEPHISTOPHELES   I am a servant to great Lucifer,

And may not follow thee without his leave.

No more than he commands must we perform.

FAUSTUS   Did not he charge thee to appear to me?

MEPHISTOPHELES   No, I came now hither of mine own accord.

FAUSTUS   Did not my conjuring speeches raise thee? Speak.

MEPHISTOPHELES   That was the cause, but yet *per accidens*.

For when we hear one rack the name of God,

Abjure the Scriptures and his Saviour Christ,

We fly in hope to get his glorious soul,

Nor will we come unless he use such means

Whereby he is in danger to be damned.

Therefore, the shortest cut for conjuring

Is stoutly to abjure all godliness,

And pray devoutly to the prince of hell.

FAUSTUS   So Faustus hath

Already done, and holds this principle:

There is no chief but only Beelzebub,

To whom Faustus doth dedicate himself.

This word 'damnation' terrifies not me,

For I confound hell in Elysium.

My ghost be with the old philosophers!

But, leaving these vain trifles of men's souls,

Tell me what is that Lucifer thy lord?

还是要海水淹没这个世界。

靡非斯特 我是伟大的撒旦的仆人，

没他的同意，不能服从你：

我们只能执行他的旨意。

浮士德 不是他命令你到这里来吗？

靡非斯特 不是，是我自愿来的。

浮士德 不是我的咒语把你招来的吗？你说！

靡非斯特 那倒也是，但也出于偶然。

当我们听见人糟蹋上帝之名，

发誓背弃《圣经》和救世主基督，

我们便飞来取他光荣的魂灵。

如果他凭此不足以下地狱，

我们也不会随意将他光顾。

因此，掌握魔法的捷径便道

就是坚决弃绝对上帝的敬仰，

并虔诚地向地狱之主祈祷。

浮士德 浮士德我已经

这样做了，我信奉的原则是：

除了别西卜，谁都不是我的主人，

我，浮士德，只为他奉献一切。

"下地狱"这话吓不倒我，

在我眼里，地狱就是乐园。

我的灵魂永远与先哲同在！

关于灵魂的废话不说也罢——

告诉我，你的主子撒旦是何人？

MEPHISTOPHELES   Arch-regent and commander of all spirits.

FAUSTUS   Was not that Lucifer an angel once?

MEPHISTOPHELES   Yes, Faustus, and most dearly loved of God.

FAUSTUS   How comes it then that he is prince of devils?

MEPHISTOPHELES   O, by aspiring pride and insolence,

For which God threw him from the face of heaven.

FAUSTUS   And what are you that live with Lucifer?

MEPHISTOPHELES   Unhappy spirits that fell with Lucifer,

Conspired against our God with Lucifer,

And are for ever damned with Lucifer.

FAUSTUS   Where are you damned?

MEPHISTOPHELES   In hell.

FAUSTUS   How comes it then that thou art out of hell?

MEPHISTOPHELES   Why, this is hell, nor am I out of it.

Think'st thou that I, who saw the face of God,

And tasted the eternal joys of heaven,

Am not tormented with ten thousand hells,

In being deprived of everlasting bliss?

O, Faustus, leave these frivolous demands,

Which strike a terror to my fainting soul!

FAUSTUS   What, is great Mephistopheles so passionate

For being deprived of the joys of heaven?

Learn thou of Faustus manly fortitude,

And scorn those joys thou never shalt possess.

Go bear these tidings to great Lucifer:

靡非斯特　他是所有精灵的头目和统帅。

浮士德　撒旦不是做过天使吗？

靡非斯特　是的，他还得过上帝的恩宠。

浮士德　他后来怎么成了魔王？

靡非斯特　哦，因为他贪图虚荣、傲慢无礼，

　　　　　　上帝就把他驱逐出了天堂。

浮士德　你们这些追随他的，又是何人？

靡非斯特　都是与他一道堕落的不幸精灵。

　　　　　　当年我等与撒旦共谋反叛上帝，

　　　　　　结果与他一起永遭天谴。

浮士德　在哪里受罚？

靡非斯特　在地狱。

浮士德　你是怎样走出地狱的？

靡非斯特　咳，这里是地狱呀！怎么出得去？

　　　　　　你想想，我曾瞻仰上帝的尊容，

　　　　　　享受天堂无穷无尽的欢乐，

　　　　　　如今永恒的幸福已被剥夺，

　　　　　　我怎能不蒙受万劫不复的痛苦？

　　　　　　哦，浮士德，别问这些鸡零狗碎了，

　　　　　　这只会使我脆弱的心徒增惶恐。

浮士德　怎么，就因天堂的欢乐被剥夺，

　　　　　　伟大的靡非斯特就如此痛苦？

　　　　　　学学浮士德男子汉的坚毅吧，

　　　　　　不属于你的欢乐不值得眷恋。

　　　　　　去吧，替我转告伟大的撒旦：

Seeing Faustus hath incurred eternal death

By desperate thoughts against Jove's deity,

Say he surrenders up to him his soul,

So he will spare him four-and-twenty years,

Letting him live in all voluptuousness,

Having thee ever to attend on me,

To give me whatsoever I shall ask,

To tell me whatsoever I demand,

To slay mine enemies and to aid my friends,

And always be obedient to my will.

Go and return to mighty Lucifer,

And meet me in my study at midnight,

And then resolve me of thy master's mind.

MEPHISTOPHELES   I will, Faustus.

     Exit [*Mephistopheles*]

FAUSTUS   Had I as many souls as there be stars,

I'd give them all for Mephistopheles.

By him I'll be great emperor of the world

And make a bridge thorough the moving air

To pass the ocean; with a band of men

I'll join the hills that bind the Afric shore,

And make that country continent to Spain,

And both contributory to my crown.

The emperor shall not live but by my leave,

Nor any potentate of Germany.

由于肆无忌惮地反对耶和华，

浮士德知道自己死后不能再生，

他甘愿向魔王交出自己的灵魂，

只要他延长他二十四年的寿命，

允许他活得快活，尽欲尽情，

并有你时时刻刻侍候左右：

我想要什么，你就给什么，

我想问什么，你就答什么，

杀死我的仇敌，帮助我的朋友，

随时随地将我的旨意奉行。

去吧，回到强大的撒旦那里，

午夜时再在我的书房相见，

向我回复你主子的旨意。

靡非斯特 遵命，浮士德。

[靡非斯特]下

浮士德 假使我的灵魂多如繁星，

为了靡非斯特，我也会悉数奉献！

有了他，我将主宰整个世界。

我要在空中架起一座大桥，

率领一大班人穿海越洋；

我要连接非洲沿海的群山，

使那里成为西班牙的内陆，

让两地都朝拜我的王冠。

没我的恩准，帝王不得施政，

德意志的君主得由我钦定。

Now that I have obtained what I desired,

I'll live in speculation of this art

Till Mephistopheles return again.

Exit [*Faustus below; exeunt Lucifer and other Devils above*]

既然我如愿以偿拥有魔法，

我就得好好揣摩其中窍门，

等到靡非斯特回到我身边。

    [浮士德]下[舞台上方的魔王偕魔鬼同下]

SCENE 4

Enter Wagner and [Robin] the Clown

WAGNER Come hither, sirrah boy.

ROBIN 'Boy'? O, disgrace to my person! Zounds, 'boy' in your face! You have seen many boys with beards, I am sure.

WAGNER Sirrah, hast thou no comings in?

ROBIN Yes, and goings out too, you may see, sir.

WAGNER Alas, poor slave, see how poverty jests in his nakedness! I know the villain's out of service, and so hungry that I know he would give his soul to the devil for a shoulder of mutton, though it were blood raw.

ROBIN Not so, neither. I had need to have it well roasted, and good sauce to it, if I pay so dear, I can tell you.

WAGNER Sirrah, wilt thou be my man and wait on me? And I will make these go like *Qui mihi discipulus*?

ROBIN What, in verse?

WAGNER No, slave, in beaten silk and stavesacre.

ROBIN Stavesacre? That's good to kill vermin. Then belike if I serve you, I shall be lousy.

WAGNER Why, so thou shalt be, whether thou dost it or no; for, sirrah,

第四场

瓦格纳偕小丑[罗宾]上

瓦格纳 过来,童儿伙计。

罗宾 "童儿",不是污辱我吗?岂有此理,去你的"童儿"!我敢说,你一定见过许多长胡须的童儿。

瓦格纳 伙计,你有收入吗?

罗宾 有啊,还有支出呢,这你看得出来的,先生。

瓦格纳 唉,真是可怜虫,穷得赤条条了还要寻开心!我知道,这家伙没有工作,没有饭吃,你只要给他一块羊肉,哪怕是血淋淋的一块,他也肯把自己的灵魂交给魔鬼。

罗宾 这不可能。我对你说,要让我付出那么高昂的代价,那块羊肉起码得烤熟,还得有上好的佐料。

瓦格纳 伙计,你愿意为我当差,为我服务吗?我会把你打扮一新,让你成为一个地道的侍童。

罗宾 你说什么,让我做"诗童"?

瓦格纳 不,奴才,是让你穿上打过边的丝绸和虮草[17]。

罗宾 虮草?那倒好,可用来除虮子。如果我为你当差,虮子就可以我为家了。

瓦格纳 不管你愿不愿意做我的差役,你身上的虮子是

41

if thou dost not presently bind thyself to me for seven years, I'll turn all the lice about thee into familiars and make then tear thee in pieces.

ROBIN   Nay, sir, you may save yourself a labour, for they are as familiar with me as if they paid for their meat and drink, I can tell you.

WAGNER   [*offering money*] Well, sirrah, leaving your jesting, and take these guilders.

ROBIN   Yes, marry, sir, and I thank you, too.

WAGNER   So, now thou art to be at an hour's warning whensoever and wheresoever the devil shall fetch thee.

ROBIN   Here, take your guiders. I'll none of ' em.

    [*He attempts to return the money*]

WAGNER   Not I. Thou art pressed. Prepare thyself, for I will presently raise up two devils to carry thee away.—Banio! Belcher!

ROBIN   Belcher?   An Belcher come here, I'll belch him. I am not afraid of a devil.

    Enter two Devils

WAGNER   [*To Robin*] How now, sir, will you serve me now?

ROBIN   Ay, good Wagner. Take away the devil, then.

WAGNER   Spirits, away!

    [*Exeunt Devils*]

Now, sirrah, follow me.

ROBIN   I will, sir. But hark you, master, will you teach me this conjuring occupation?

少不了的。伙计,如果你不赶紧跟我签订契约,为我
服务七年,那我就要让虱子来跟你套近乎,把你撕成
碎片。

罗宾　先生,这倒不劳你自个儿费心,虱子早已跟我混熟
了。我可以告诉你, 它们一直在我身上随便吃肉喝
酒,和付过账似的呢。

瓦格纳　[给钱]好了,伙计,别说笑了,收好这几个银
角子。

罗宾　是,先生,多谢多谢。

瓦格纳　记住:无论什么时候,什么地方,即便魔鬼找你,
你也得随叫随到,听候我的吩咐。

罗宾　这几个银角子你拿回去吧。我一个子儿都不要了。

　　　　[他试图还钱]

瓦格纳　我不拿回,你只能收下。你等着,我马上招两个
魔鬼来,把你抓了去。——班尼奥、贝尔契!

罗宾　贝尔契?如果贝尔契来了,我要先揍他一顿。我可
不怕魔鬼。

　　　　二魔鬼上

瓦格纳　[对罗宾]怎么样,伙计,现在愿意为我当差了吧?

罗宾　好瓦格纳,快让魔鬼走吧。

瓦格纳　精灵,去!

　　　　[二魔鬼下]

好了,伙计,跟上我吧。

罗宾　好的,先生。我说,主人,你能教教我这个招鬼的法
术吗?

WAGNER Ay, sirrah, I'll teach thee to turn thyself to a dog, or a cat, or a mouse, or a rat, or anything.

ROBIN   A dog, or a cat, or a mouse, or a rat? O brave, Wagner!

WAGNER   Villain, call me Master Wagner, and see that you walk attentively, and let your right eye be always diametrally fixed upon my left heel, that thou mayest *quasi vestgiis nostris insistere*.

ROBIN   Well, sir, I warrant you.

Exeunt

瓦格纳 好,我可以先教你如何把自己变成一条狗,或者一只猫,一只老鼠什么的。

罗宾 变成狗,或者猫和老鼠？哟,了不起的瓦格纳!

瓦格纳 混蛋,你得叫我瓦格纳大师。走路时要小心,右眼要紧盯我的左脚跟,这样才能步我的后尘,踏我的脚印。

罗宾 是,先生,这没问题。

　　　　瓦格纳偕罗宾下

ACT 2

第二幕

SCENE 1

Enter Faustus in his study

FAUSTUS Now, Faustus, must thou needs be damned?

Canst thou not be saved?

What boots it then to think of God or heaven?

Away with such vain fancies, and despair!

Despair in God and trust in Beelzebub.

Now go not backward, Faustus, be resolute.

Why waver'st thou? O, something soundeth in mine ears:

'Abjure this magic, turn to God again!'

Why, he loves thee not.

The god thou serv'st is thine own appetite,

Wherein is fixed the love of Beelzebub.

To him I'll build an altar and a church,

And offer lukewarm blood of new-born babes.

Enter the two Angels

BAD ANGEL Go forward, Faustus, in that famous art.

GOOD ANGEL Sweet Faustus, leave that execrable art.

FAUSTUS Contrition, prayer, repentance—what of these?

GOOD ANGEL O, they are means to bring thee unto heaven.

第一场

　　　　　　　浮士德在书斋里

浮士德　浮士德啊,你必遭天谴了吧?

　　　　你还能有救赎的希望吗?

　　　　这时才想到上帝和天堂,有用吗?

　　　　别胡思乱想了,你就绝望去吧!

　　　　对上帝绝望,对魔鬼信心满满!

　　　　别退缩了,浮士德,坚强些。

　　　　为何犹豫?哦,耳边好像有个声音:

　　　　"丢开魔术,回到上帝身边来!"

　　　　但上帝已经不爱你了。

　　　　你侍奉的上帝是自己的欲望,

　　　　你的爱已经献给魔王撒旦。

　　　　我要为他建起祭坛和教堂,

　　　　为他献上婴儿温暖的血浆。

　　　　　　　二天使上

坏天使　浮士德,继续这非凡的法术吧。

好天使　浮士德,放弃这邪恶的妖术吧。

浮士德　悔悟、祈祷、赎罪——好处何在?

好天使　哦,这是引领你上天堂的路。

BAD ANGEL Rather illusions, fruits of lunacy,

That make them foolish that do trust them most.

GOOD ANGEL Sweet Faustus, think of heaven and heavenly things.

BAD ANGEL No, Faustus, think of honour and of wealth.

Exeunt Angels

FAUSTUS Wealth!

Why, the seigniory of Emden shall be mine.

When Mephistopheles shall stand by me,

What power can hurt me? Faustus, thou art safe;

Cast no more doubts.Mephistopheles, come,

And bring glad tidings from great Lucifer.

Is't not midnight? Come, Mephistopheles!

Veni, veni, Mephistophile!

Enter Mephistopheles

Now tell me what saith Lucifer thy lord?

MEPHISTOPHELES That I shall wait on Faustus whilst he lives,

So he will buy my service with his soul.

FAUSTUS Already Faustus hath hazarded that for thee.

MEPHISTOPHELES But now thou must bequeath it solemnly

And write a deed of gift with thine own blood,

For that security craves great Lucifer.

If thou deny it, I must back to hell.

FAUSTUS Stay, Mephistopheles, and tell me,

What good will my soul do thy lord?

MEPHISTOPHELES Enlarge his kingdom.

坏天使　这只是幻想,精神错乱的产物,

只能让信奉者越发糊涂。

好天使　亲爱的浮士德,想想天堂和天上的幸福。

坏天使　别想那些,浮士德,应想想荣誉和财富。

　　　　二天使下

浮士德　财富?

是呀,埃姆登[18]就是我的领地了。

靡非斯特一旦为我效劳,

谁还能伤害我?浮士德是安全的;

别再迟疑了,来吧,靡非斯特!

从魔王那里给我带来好消息。

现在已是子夜,来吧,靡非斯特!

来吧,来吧,靡非斯特!

　　　　靡非斯特上

告诉我,你的主人撒旦怎么说?

靡非斯特　他说,浮士德拿灵魂换取我的服务,

只要他活着一天,服务就不终止。

浮士德　为得到你的服务,我甘愿冒风险。

靡非斯特　但你还得办个庄严的手续:

用你自己的血写一纸文书,

魔王撒旦需要这份担保。

如果你拒绝,我即刻返回地狱。

浮士德　等一等,靡非斯特,告诉我:

你的主子取我灵魂有何用处?

靡非斯特　扩张他的王国。

FAUSTUS   Is that the reason why he tempts us thus?

MEPHISTOPHELES   *Solamen miseris socios habuisse doloris.*

FAUSTUS   Why, have you any pain, that torture others!

MEPHISTOPHELES   As great as have the human souls of men.

But, tell me, Faustus, shall I have thy soul?

And I will be thy slave, and wait on thee,

And give thee more than thou hast wit to ask.

FAUSTUS   Ay, Mephistopheles, I give it him.

MEPHISTOPHELES   Then, Faustus, stab thine arm courageously,

And bind thy soul that at some certain day

Great Lucifer may claim it as his own,

And then be thou as great as Lucifer.

FAUSTUS   [*cutting his arm*]

Lo, Mephistopheles, for love of thee

Faustus hath cut his arm, and with his proper blood

Assures my soul to be great Lucifer's,

Chief lord and regent of perpetual night.

View here the blood that trickles from mine arm,

And let it be propitious for my wish.

MEPHISTOPHELES   But, Faustus,

Write it in manner of a deed of gift.

FAUSTUS   Ay, so I do. [*He writes*] But, Mephistopheles,

My blood congeals, and I can write no more.

MEPHISTOPHELES   I'll fetch thee fire to dissolve it straight.

Exit [*Mephistopheles*]

浮士德　这就是他诱惑我们的理由？

靡非斯特　患难者互为伙伴，不失为安慰。

浮士德　怎么，你们折磨别人，也有痛苦？

靡非斯特　与人类一样，我们也创巨痛深。

　　　　　告诉我，我能得到你的灵魂吗？

　　　　　我愿意做奴隶，忠心服侍你，

　　　　　你能得到的，将超过你的预期。

浮士德　靡非斯特，我愿意把灵魂交给撒旦。

靡非斯特　好，浮士德，勇敢地刺破手臂，

　　　　　明确写下交出灵魂的日期，

　　　　　好让魔王届时占为己有，

　　　　　那时你将与他一样伟大无比。

浮士德　［浮士德刺破手臂］

　　　　　看，靡非斯特，为了你的爱，

　　　　　浮士德已将手臂割开，凭这血，

　　　　　我保证将灵魂交给伟大的魔王，

　　　　　永恒黑夜的主人和统治者。

　　　　　看，血从我的手臂汩汩流淌，

　　　　　但愿顺畅的还有我的希望。

靡非斯特　浮士德，

　　　　　按赠予契约的格式写吧。

浮士德　好，我就写。［写契约］但靡非斯特，

　　　　　我的血凝固了，再写不下去。

靡非斯特　我马上去取火，将凝固的血化开。

　　　　　　　［靡非斯特下］

53

FAUSTUS   What might the staying of my blood portend?

Is it unwilling I should write this bill?

Why streams it not, that I may write afresh?

'Faustus gives to thee his soul'—O, there it stayed!

Why shouldst thou not? is not thy soul thine own?

Then write again: 'Faustus gives to thee his soul.'

Enter Mephistopheles with the chafer of fire

MEPHISTOPHELES   See, Faustus, here's fire. Set it on.

FAUSTUS   So. Now the blood begins to clear again.

Now will I make an end immediately.

[*He writes*]

MEPHISTOPHELES   [*aside*]

What will not I do to obtain his soul?

FAUSTUS   *Consummatum est.* This bill is ended,

And Faustus hath bequeathed his soul to Lucifer

But what is this inscription on mine arm?

'*Homo, fuge!* ' Whither should I fly?

If unto heaven, he'll throw me down to hell.—

My senses are deceived; here's nothing writ.—

O, yes, I see it plain. Even here is writ

'*Homo, fuge!* ' yet shall not Faustus fly.

MEPHISTOPHELES   [*aside*]

I'll fetch him somewhat to delight his mind.

Exit [*Mephistopheles*]. *Enter Devils, giving crowns and
rich apparel to Faustus; thay dance, and then depart. Enter*

54

浮士德　我的血凝固了,这是什么兆头?

　　难道神明不愿我签署这份契约?

　　血为何不流? 为何不让我写下去?

　　"浮士德将灵魂交出"——就停在这里!

　　怎么不能交? 难道灵魂不属于我自己?

　　再试试:"浮士德将灵魂交出。"

　　　　靡非斯特捧火盆重上

靡非斯特　浮士德,火来了,放上面烘烘。

浮士德　好。凝血开始溶化了。

　　我得赶紧将最后几句写下来。

　　　　[写]

靡非斯特　[旁白]

　　为取他的灵魂,让我干什么都行。

浮士德　成了! 契约终于写好了。

　　浮士德已将灵魂赠予撒旦。

　　咳,我手臂上怎么出现了文字?

　　"人啊,逃吧! "[19]我能逃往哪里?

　　若逃往天堂,主会将我赶回地狱——

　　我神志不清了,这里并没有文字——

　　哎呀,有的,写得清清楚楚,这边还有:

　　"人啊,逃吧! "浮士德不想逃走。

靡非斯特　[旁白]

　　我去叫几个魔鬼来,让他高兴起来。

　　　　[靡非斯特]下。少顷,众魔鬼上,向浮士德献上
　　　　王冠和华服;众魔鬼跳舞,然后散去。靡非斯特

Mephistopheles

FAUSTUS   What means this show?   Speak, Mephistopheles.

MEPHISTOPHELES   Nothing, Faustus, but to delight thy mind

And let thee see what magic can perform.

FAUSTUS   But may I raise such spirits when I please?

MEPHISTOPHELES   Ay, Faustus, and do greater things than these.

FAUSTUS   Then Mephistopheles, receive this scroll,

A deed of gift of body and of soul—

But yet conditionally that thou perform

All covenants and articles between us both.

MEPHISTOPHELES   Faustus, I swear by hell and Lucifer

To effect all promises between us both.

FAUSTUS   Then hear me read it, Mephistopheles.

'On these conditions following:

First, that Faustus may be a spirit in form and substance.

Secondly, that Mephistopheles shall be his servant, and at his command.

Thirdly, that Mephistopheles shall do for him, and bring him whatsoever he desires.

Fourthly, that he shall be in his chamber or house invisible.

Lastly, that he shall appear to the said John Faustus at all times in what shape or form soever he please.

I, John Faustus, of Wittenberg, Doctor, by these presents, do give both body and soul to Lucifer, Prince of the East, and his minister Mephistopheles; and furthermore grant unto them that twenty-four

重上。

浮士德 这场表演是什么意思？靡非斯特,你说。

靡非斯特 没什么,浮士德,只是想让你高兴,

让你看看魔法是何等神奇。

浮士德 我能随便召唤这些精灵么?

靡非斯特 当然,浮士德,还有比这更神奇的呢。

浮士德 靡非斯特,请收好这份文书,

这是赠予肉体和灵魂的契约。

我有话在先:我们签订的这份契约,

包括其中的条款,你得切实履行。

靡非斯特 浮士德,我凭地狱和撒旦起誓,

这里的承诺,我一定如实兑现。

浮士德 听我念一遍吧,靡非斯特,

条款的细则如下:

其一:浮士德可以具有精灵的形体与特质;

其二:靡非斯特应充当他的仆人,并听他的使唤;

其三:浮士德想做什么,想得到什么,靡非斯特应当遂他所愿;

其四:靡非斯特可以隐身在浮士德的房间里或住宅中;

最后一款:无论什么时候,只要浮士德开口,靡非斯特都必须按他所吩咐的面目现身。

我,来自维腾堡的约翰·浮士德博士,凭本契约将自己的肉体和灵魂交给东方之王撒旦和他的大臣靡非斯特;二十四年以后,如果上述条款履

years being expired, and these articles above written being inviolate, full power to fetch or carry the said John Faustus, body and soul, flesh, blood, into their habitation wheresoever.

By me, John Faustus'

MEPHISTOPHELES   Speak, Faustus. Do you deliver this as your deed?

FAUSTUS   [*giving the deed*] Ay. Take it, and the devil give thee good of it!

MEPHISTOPHELES   So. Now, Faustus, ask me what thou wilt.

FAUSTUS   First I will question thee about hell.

Tell me, where is the place that men call hell?

MEPHISTOPHELES   Under the heavens.

FAUSTUS   Ay, so are all things else. But whereabouts?

MEPHISTOPHELES   Within the bowels of these elements,

Where we are tortured and remain for ever.

Hell hath no limits, nor is circumscribed

In one self place, but where we are is hell,

And where hell is there must we ever be.

And, to be short, when all the world dissolves,

And every creature shall be purified,

All places shall be hell that are not heaven.

FAUSTUS   I think hell's a fable.

MEPHISTOPHELES   Ay, think so still, till experience change thy mind.

FAUSTUS   Why, dost thou think that Faustus shall be damned?

MEPHISTOPHELES   Ay, of necessity, for here's the scroll

In which thou hast given thy soul to Lucifer.

FAUSTUS   Ay, and body too. But what of that?

58

行无误,他们将完全有权把立约人约翰·浮士德的躯体和灵魂,连同血与肉,带去他们所居住的任何地方。

约翰·浮士德(签名画押)

靡非斯特 浮士德,这就是你递呈的契约么?

浮士德 [递过契约]正是。请收下,魔王保佑你。

靡非斯特 好,浮士德,你现在可以提要求了。

浮士德 首先,我要问问你有关地狱的情况:

告诉我,人们所说的地狱在哪里?

靡非斯特 在苍天底下。

浮士德 万物都在苍天底下。但地狱到底在哪里?

靡非斯特 在各种元素的内脏中。

我们就在那里受折磨,永远留居。

地狱没有边界,也没有范围,

我们出现在哪里,哪里就是地狱,

地狱就是我们的必然之所。

简言之,在这世界消亡以前,

所有的生灵涤清罪孽以前,

除了天堂,其他地方均为地狱。

浮士德 我觉得地狱不过是无稽之谈。

靡非斯特 你怎么想都行,但经验会让你改变想法。

浮士德 你认为浮士德会遭天谴吗?

靡非斯特 那是必然的,凭这一纸文书,

你的灵魂已经赠予撒旦。

浮士德 不错,包括肉体。这有什么要紧?

Think'st thou that Faustus is so fond to imagine

That after this life there is any pain?

No, these are trifles and mere old wives' tales.

MEPHISTOPHELES   But I am an instance to prove the contrary,

For I tell thee I am damned and am now in hell.

FAUSTUS   Nay, an this be hell, I'll willingly be damned.

What? Sleeping, eating, walking, disputing?

But leaving this, let me have a wife, the fairest maid in Germany,

For I am wanton and lascivious and cannot live without a wife.

MEPHISTOPHELES   Well, Faustus, thou shalt have a wife.

He fetches in a women Devil

FAUSTUS   What sight is this?

MEPHISTOPHELES   Now, Faustus, wilt thou have a wife?

FAUSTUS   Here's a hot whore indeed! No, I'll no wife.

MEPHISTOPHELES   Marriage is but a ceremonial toy.

An if thou lovest me, think no more of it.

[*Exit Devil*]

I'll cull thee out the fairest courtesans

And bring them every morning to thy bed.

She whom thine eye shall like, thy heart shall have,

Be she as chaste as was Penelope,

As wise as Saba, or as beautiful

As was bright Lucifer before his fall.

[*presenting a book*]

Here, take this book and peruse it well.

你以为浮士德就那么天真，

会相信人死后还会有痛苦？

没有的，那是老婆子们的无稽之言。

靡非斯特 我自己就是地狱存在的见证，

告诉你，我就因遭了天谴才在地狱安身。

浮士德 如果这样吃吃睡睡，走着路，说着话，

就是地狱，我倒乐意遭受天谴。

闲话少说，给我找个妻子来，必须是全德国最美的女

子，我天生放荡好色，没有女人可活不下去。

靡非斯特 好，浮士德，你马上就有妻子。

靡非斯特招一女鬼上

浮士德 这女人怎么这样难看？

靡非斯特 浮士德，你不是要一个妻子么？

浮士德 这是个烂婊子。我不要妻子了。

靡非斯特 婚姻不过是一场仪式性的游戏。

如果你把我当朋友，这事别再想了。

[女鬼下]

我要为你挑选最漂亮的姑娘，

每天早上把她送到你的床前。

让你眼中流露喜悦，内心念念不忘。

给你的姑娘个个纯洁如珀涅罗珀[20]，

聪明如示巴女王[21]，论外表的美貌，

比得上堕落前那光芒四射的撒旦。

[递给浮士德一册书]

这册书你拿着，好好读一读，

The iterating of these lines brings gold;

The framing of this circle on the ground

Brings thunder, whirlwinds, storm, and lightning.

Pronounce this thrice devoutly to thyself,

And men in harness shall appear to thee

Ready to execute what thou command'st.

FAUSTUS   Thanks, Mephistopheles, for this sweet book.

This will I keep as chary as my life.

Exeunt

念念书中的句子就能获得金子，
在地上画个圈，天空就会出闪电，
雷电交加，刮起大风，暴雨倾盆。
书上这句咒语，虔诚地念上五遍，
全副武装的兵士就来到你面前，
随时准备执行你的号令。

浮士德　这真是本好书，谢谢，靡非斯特，
我会好好保管，视它为生命。

　　同下

SCENE 2

Enter [Robin] the Clown [with a conjuring book]

ROBIN   *[calling offstage]* What, Dick, look to the horses there till I come again.—I have gotten one of Doctor Faustus' conjuring books, and now we'll have such knavery as't passes.

     Enter Dick

DICK   What, Robin, you must come away and walk the horses.

ROBIN   I walk the horses? I scorn't, 'faith. I have other matters in hand. Let the horses walk themselves an they will. *[He reads]* 'A' *per se* 'a'; 't', 'h', 'e', 'the'; 'o' *per se* 'o'; 'deny orgon, gorgon'. —Keep further from me, O thou illiterate and unlearned ostler.

DICK   Snails, what hast thou got there, a book? Why, thou canst not tell ne'er a word on't.

ROBIN   That thou shalt see presently. *[He draws a circle]* Keep out of the circle, I say, lest I send you into the hostry, with a vengeance.

DICK   That's like, 'faith! You had best leave your foolery, for an my master come he'll conjure you, 'faith.

ROBIN   My masters conjure me? I'll tell thee what: an my master come here, I'll clap as fair as a pair of horns on's head as e'er thou sawest in thy life.

第二场

小丑[罗宾手握一魔法书]上

罗宾 ［朝后台］狄克,你把马看管好,我过一会过去。
——我拿来了一本浮士德博士的魔法书,现在我要
试试这套把戏。

狄克上

狄克 罗宾,你得去遛马了。

罗宾 我去遛马?我才不干呢。我手头有事,让马自个儿
遛去吧。[念]"A即为A,而t、h、e组成了the;O即为O,
狄摩——奥根,高根"——离我远点,你这没文化、没
教养的马夫。

狄克 蜗牛,你拿着的是书吗?怎么,上面的字你一个也
不认得?

罗宾 你等着瞧吧。[画一圆圈]离这圈子远点。我警告
你,否则我一个咒语把你送回马厩。

狄克 这倒有可能。别再干傻事了,如果让我的主人[22]看
见,他会把你的魂勾走的,我保证。

罗宾 勾我的魂?我告诉你:如果我的主人在这里,我会
敲敲他头上那对角,那可是你从未见过的一对最漂
亮的大角。

DICK   Thou need'st not do that, for my mistress hath done it.

ROBIN   Ay, there be of us here that have waded as deep into matters as other men, if they were disposed to talk.

DICK   A plague take you! I thought you did not sneak up and down after her for nothing. But I prithee tell me in good sadness, Robin, is that a conjuring book?

ROBIN   Do but speak what thou'lt have me to do, and I'll do't. If thou'lt dance naked, put off thy clothes, and I'll conjure thee about presently. Or if thou'lt go but to the tarven with me, I'll give thee white wine, red wine, claret wine, sack, muscadine, malmsey, and whippincrust, hold belly hold, and we'll not pay one penny for it.

DICK   O brave! Prithee let's to it presently, for I am as dry ad a dog.

ROBIN   Come, theen, let's away.

Exeunt

狄克　这你用不着费心,我的女主人自己已经敲过了。[23]

罗宾　嗨,我跟别人一样,遇到这种事,总喜欢深深地插上一竿子。

狄克　你遭瘟去吧! 我知道你鬼鬼祟祟地跟在她后面,不会有好事。但我还是要一本正经地恳求你告诉我,罗宾,那真是一本魔法书吗?

罗宾　就说你要我做点什么吧,我会尽力的。如果你想赤身裸体地跳个舞,我马上在你身上施魔法。如果你想跟我上酒店,我会变出白烧、红烧、红葡萄酒、白葡萄酒、麝香葡萄酒、烈性白葡萄甜酒、威宾克拉斯特酒,你可以解开裤带喝,一个子儿也不用付。

狄克　好哇好哇! 我们马上就去,你说得我喉咙冒烟了。

罗宾　那就走吧。

　　　　同下

SCENE 3

Enter Faustus in his study, and Mephistopheles

FAUSTUS   When I behold the heavens, then I repent,

And curse thee, wicked Mephistopheles,

Because thou hast deprived me of those joys.

MEPHISTOPHELES   'Twas thine own seeking, Faustus. Thanks thyself.

But think'st thou heaven is such a glorious thing?

I tell thee, Faustus, it is not half so fair

As thou or any man that breathes on earth.

FAUSTUS   How prov'st thou that?

MEPHISTOPHELES   'Twas made for man; then he's more excellent.

FAUSTUS   If heaven was made for man, 'twas made for me.

I will renounce this magic and repent.

Enter the two Angels

GOOD ANGEL   Faustus, repent! Yet God will pity thee.

BAD ANGEL   Thou art a spirit. God cannot pity thee.

FAUSTUS   Who buzzeth in mine ears I am a spirit?

Be I a devil, yet God may pity me;

Yea, God will pity me, if I repent.

BAD ANGEL   Ay, but Faustus never shall repent.

第三场

浮士德、靡非斯特在书房里

浮士德 可恶的靡非斯特,当我仰望天空,

我便心怀悔恨,只想诅咒你,

因为你夺去了我天堂的快乐。

靡非斯特 那是你自找的,浮士德,感谢你自己吧。

你真的觉得天堂是你的福地吗?

我告诉你,浮士德,那里并不好,

远不如活在尘世的你和其他人。

浮士德 何以见得?

靡非斯特 天堂是为人创造的,因为人更优越。

浮士德 既然为人所创造,那就是为我而创造的。

我要声明放弃魔法,诚心忏悔。

二天使上

好天使 浮士德,忏悔吧! 上帝还怜悯着你。

坏天使 你已是精灵,上帝不会怜悯你。

浮士德 谁在我耳边嘁嘁叫,说我是精灵?

即便我是魔鬼,上帝也会怜悯我;

是的,只要我诚心忏悔,上帝就会怜悯我。

坏天使 是的,但浮士德永远不会忏悔。

Exeunt Angels

FAUSTUS   My heart is hardened; I cannot repent.

Scarce can I name salvation, faith, or heaven,

Swords, poison, halters, and envenomed steel

Are laid before me to despatch myself;

And long ere this I should have done the deed,

Had not sweet pleasure conquered deep despair.

Have not I made blind Homer sing to me

Of Alexander's love and Oenone's death?

And hath not he that built the walls of Thebes

With ravishing sound of his melodious harp

Made music with my Mephistopheles?

Why should I die, then, or basely despair?

I am resolved; Faustus shall ne'er repent.

Come, Mephistopheles, let us dispute again

And reason of divine astrology.

Speak. Are there many spheres above the moon?

Are all celestial bodies but one globe,

As is the substance of this centric earth?

MEPHISTOPHELES   As are the elements, such are the heavens,

Even from the moon unto the empyreal orb,

Mutually folded in each other's spheres,

All jointly move upon one axletree,

Whose termine is termed the world's wide pole.

Nor are the names of Saturn, Mars, or Jupiter

二天使下

浮士德　我的心肠硬如铁石;我不可能忏悔。

救赎、信仰和天堂,我都不愿提起。

刀斧、毒药和绞索摆在我面前,

我随时可用来结束自己的性命。

要不是甜美的欢愉征服了绝望,

我早就自寻短见,一命呜呼。

我召唤瞎眼的荷马为我歌唱

帕里斯的爱情和俄诺涅[24]的死亡;

曾用琴音修筑底比斯城墙的那个人

跟我的靡非斯特一道

为我弹奏优美动人的乐章。

我干吗要死？何必这般悲观？

浮士德想好了,他决不忏悔。

来吧,靡非斯特,我们继续讨论

神圣的占星术,说说它的必要性。

你说,月球之上还有星球吗？

是不是所有的天体都是圆球状的,

论实质与我们的大地没有两样？

靡非斯特　从月球到最高天,凡天体

都由水、火、气、土诸元素构成。

它们自成一体,相互环绕,

围着同一个轴干不断运转,

轴的尽头叫作世界之极。

所谓的土星、火星和木星,

Feigned, but are erring stars.

FAUSTUS   But have they all one motion, both *situ et tempore*?

MEPHISTOPHELES   All move from east to west in twenty-four hours upon the poles of the world, but differ in their motion upon the poles of the zodiac.

FAUSTUS   These slender trifles Wagner can decide.

Hath Mephistopheles no greater skill?

Who knows not the double motion of the planets?

That the first is finished in a natural day,

The second thus: Saturn in thirty years, Jupiter in twelve, Mars in four, the sun, Venus, and Mercury in a year, the moon in twenty-eight days. These are freshmen's questions. But, tell me, hath every sphere a dominion or *intelligentia*?

MEPHISTOPHELES   Ay.

FAUSTUS   How many heavens or spheres are there?

MEPHISTOPHELES   Nine: the seven planets, the firmament, and the empyreal heaven.

FAUSTUS   But is there not *coelum igneum et crystallinum*?

MEPHISTOPHELES   No, Fautus, they be but fables.

FAUSTUS   Resolve me then in this one question: why are not conjunctions, oppositions, aspects, eclipses all at one time, but in some years we have more, in some less?

MEPHISTOPHELES   *Per inoequalem motum respectu totius.*

FAUSTUS   Well, I am answered. Now tell me who made the world.

MEPHISTOPHELES   I will not.

也非虚构,都是运行着的星球。

浮士德 它们在时空中运行是否一致?

靡非斯特 这些星球在二十四小时内由东至西沿着
赤道移动,但它们在黄道带上的运行轨迹并非
一致。

浮士德 这些鸡零狗碎,瓦格纳也说得清楚。
靡非斯特就没有更大的能耐了吗?
行星运行的双重性,谁不知道?
第一种运行在二十四小时内完成,
第二种运行:土星是三十年,木星是十二年,火星是
四年,太阳、金星和水星都是一年,月亮则为二十八
天。这是大学一年级生都能掌握的常识。跟我说说:
是不是每个天体的背后都有一个司事天使?

靡非斯特 是的。

浮士德 天或者说天体,共有几层?

靡非斯特 九层:七大行星各占一层,加上恒星层,以及
最高天。

浮士德 就没有火焰层和水晶层吗?

靡非斯特 没有,浮士德,那都是虚构的。

浮士德 为我解答这一问题:为什么星球的轨道相交、方
向相背、相对位置和晦蚀现象,并不同时发生,有些
年份出现得多一些,有些年份少一些?

靡非斯特 因为所有星球运行的速度并不相同。

浮士德 好,就算是吧。告诉我:这个世界是谁创造的?

靡非斯特 这我不能说。

FAUSTUS   Sweet Mephistopheles, tell me.

MEPHISTOPHELES   Move me not, Faustus.

FAUSTUS   Villain, have I not bound thee to tell me any thing?

MEPHISTOPHELES   Ay, that is not against our kingdom.

This is. Thou art damned. Think thou of hell.

FAUSTUS   Think, Faustus, upon God, that made the world.

MEPHISTOPHELES   Remember this.

Exit [Mephistopheles]

FAUSTUS   Ay, go, accursed spirit, to ugly hell!

'Tis thou hast damned distressed Faustus' soul.

Is't not too late?

Enter the two Angels

BAD ANGEL   Too late.

GOOD ANGEL   Never too late, if Faustus can repent.

BAD ANGEL   If thou repent, devils shall tear thee in pieces.

GOOD ANGEL   Repent, and they shall never raze thy skin.

Exeunt Angels

FAUSTUS   O Christ, my Saviour, my Saviour,

Help to save distressed Faustus' soul!

Enter Lucifer, Belzebub, and Mephistopheles

LUCIFER   Christ cannot save thy soul, for he is just.

There's none but I have interest in the same.

FAUSTUS   O, what art thou that look'st so terribly?

LUCIFER   I am Lucifer,

And this is my companion prince in hell.

74

浮士德　亲爱的靡非斯特,告诉我。

靡非斯特　别逼我了,浮士德。

浮士德　混蛋! 不是事先约定你得答应我所要求的一切吗?

靡非斯特　是的,但前提是不冒犯我们的王国。

　　　这一要求就是冒犯了。你已遭天谴,想想地狱吧。

浮士德　浮士德啊,想想创造世界的上帝吧。

靡非斯特　记住我的话。

　　　　靡非斯特下

浮士德　该死的魔鬼,滚吧,到丑恶的地狱里去!

　　　正是你让不幸的浮士德遭受天谴。

　　　现在忏悔,是不是为时太晚了?

　　　　二天使上

坏天使　太晚了。

好天使　只要浮士德愿意忏悔,永远不晚。

坏天使　如果你忏悔,魔鬼会把你撕成碎片!

好天使　忏悔吧,魔鬼动不了你一根毫毛。

　　　　二天使下

浮士德　基督啊,我的救星,我的救星!

　　　救救不幸的浮士德的灵魂吧!

　　　　撒旦、别西卜上。靡非斯特重上

撒旦　基督不可能拯救你的灵魂,因为他是公正的。

　　　对你的灵魂感兴趣的,除了我不会有其他的神。

浮士德　哟,你是谁? 长得如此恐怖!

撒旦　我是撒旦。

　　　这是与我一道掌管地狱的一位王子。

FAUSTUS   O, Faustus, they are come to fetch away thy soul!

BEELZEBUB   We come to tell thee thou dost injure us.

LUCIFER   Thou call'st of Christ, contrary to thy promise.

BEELZEBUB   Thou shouldst not think on God.

LUCIFER   Think on the devil.

BEELZEBUB   And of his dam, too.

FAUSTUS   Nor will I henceforth. Pardon him in this, and Faustus vows never to look to heaven.

LUCIFER   So shalt thou show thyself an obedient servant, and we will highly gratify thee for it.

BEELZEBUB   Faustus, we are come from hell to show thee some pastime. Sit down, and thou shalt behold all the Seven Deadly Sins appear in their proper shapes and likeness.

FAUSTUS   That sight will be as pleasant to me as paradise was to Adam the first day of his creation.

LUCIFER   Talk not of paradise nor creation, but mark this show. Go, Mephistopheles, fetch them in.

> [*Faustus sits, and Mephistopheles fetches the Sins.*] *Enter the Seven Deadly Sins*

BEELZEBUB   Now, Faustus, examine them of their several names and dispositions.

FAUSTUS   That shall be soon.—What art thou, the first?

PRIDE   I am Pride. I disdain to have any parents. I am like to Ovid's flea: I can creep into every corner of a wench. Sometimes like a periwig I sit upon her brow; next, like a necklace I hang about her neck;

浮士德　浮士德啊,他们来取你的灵魂了。

别西卜　我们是来告诉你:你伤害了我们。

撒旦　你呼唤基督,违背了自己的承诺。

别西卜　你不应该想着上帝。

撒旦　你应该想着魔鬼。

别西卜　以及他的诅咒。

浮士德　以后浮士德不想上帝了。原谅我这一次,浮士德
　　向你们保证,从此再不仰望天空了。

撒旦　只要你诚心诚意归顺我们, 我们将让你获得最大
　　的满足。

别西卜　浮士德, 我们亲自从地狱赶来, 是想给你解解
　　闷。坐下,你将看到七大罪孽以他们的真面目出现在
　　你面前。

浮士德　这样的场面定能让我赏心悦目, 就像被创造的
　　亚当第一天见到天堂一样。

撒旦　别提天堂和创造,仔细观看就是。靡非斯特,去,把他
　　们叫进来。

　　　　[浮士德落座。靡非斯特传唤七大罪孽。]七大罪
　　　　孽上

别西卜　浮士德,你现在就问问他们吧:什么名字,有什
　　么爱好。

浮士德　我这就问。——第一位,你是谁?

骄傲　我是骄傲。我觉得人不需要有父母。就像奥维德笔
　　下的跳蚤,我总能在放荡女人的身体上到处爬。有时
　　我像她头上戴的假发;有时又像她脖子上挂着的项

then, like a fan of feathers I kiss her, and then, turning myself to a wrought smock, do what I list. But fie, what a smell is here! I'll not speak a word more for a king's ransom, unless the ground be perfumed and covered with cloth of arras.

FAUSTUS   Thou art a proud knave, indeed.—What art thou, the second?

COVETOUSNESS   I am Covetousness, begotten of an old churl in a leathern bag; and might I now obtain my wish, this house, you, and all should turn to gold, that I might lock you safe into my chest. O my sweet gold!

FAUSTUS   And what art thou, the third?

ENVY   I am Envy, begotten of a chimney-sweeper and an oyster-wife. I cannot read, and therefore wish all books were burnt. I am lean with seeing others eat. O, that there would come a famine through all the world, that all might die and I live alone! Then thou shouldst see how fat I'd be. But must thou sit and I stand? Come down, with a vengeance!

FAUSTUS   Out, envious wretch!—But what art thou, the fourth?

WRATH   I am Wrath. I had neither father nor mother. I leaped out of a lion's mouth when I was scarce an hour old, and ever since have run up and down the world with these case of rapiers, wounding myself when I could get none to fight withal. I was born in hell, and look to it, for some of you shall be my father.

FAUSTUS   And what art thou, the fifth?

GLUTTONY   I am Gluttony. My parents are all dead, and the devil a penny they have left me but a small pension, and that buys me thirty

链。有时我是一把羽毛扇,亲吻着她的脸;有时不啻为披在她身上一件漂亮的罩衣。总之,我随心所欲,什么都敢做。呸! 这里有什么气味! 我不想再说了,给我金山银山也不说,除非地上洒满香水,铺起漂亮的花毯。

浮士德 你确实是个骄傲的恶棍。——第二位,你是谁?

贪婪 我是贪婪,出生在一个皮袋里,生父是个守财奴。如果让我心满意足,这幢房子连同你们这班人,都应该变成金子,那时我就可以把你们当作我的财物,安全地锁进箱子里。我可爱的金子啊!

浮士德 第三位,你是谁?

妒忌 我是妒忌,父亲扫烟囱,母亲是个卖牡蛎的女贩子。我不识字,巴不得放一把火烧光所有书籍。看别人吃喝,我因此长瘦了。我真恨不得全世界发生大饥荒,所有的人都饿死,就我一个人活着。那时你一定能看见我长成了胖子。为什么你可以坐着,而我得站在这里?一骨碌滚下来吧!

浮士德 去,真是个好妒忌的恶棍! ——第四位,你是谁?

愤怒 我是愤怒。我没有父母。我来到人世不到一小时,便从狮子嘴里跳出,从此以后,我便手提这把宝剑奔走于世间,找不到决斗的对手时,我就用它刺伤我自己。我是地狱出生的,那地方我要随时留意,因为你们当中的某一个说不定就是我的父亲。

浮士德 你是谁,第五位?

饕餮 我是饕餮。我的父母都死了,他们一个子儿也没有留给我,只有一笔小小的年金,只够我一天吃三

meals a day, and ten bevers—a small trifle to suffice nature. I come of a royal pedigree! My father was a gammon of bacon, and my mother was a hogshead of claret wine. My godfathers were these: Peter Pickle-herring and Martin Martlemas-beef. But my godmother, O, she was an ancient gentlewoman; her name was Mistress Margery March-beer. Now, Faustus, thou hast heard all my progeny, wilt thou bid me to supper?

FAUSTUS Not I.

GLUTTONY Then the devil choke thee!

FAUSTUS Choke thyself, glutton!—What art thou, the sixth?

SLOTH Heigh-ho. I am Sloth. I was begotten on a sunny bank. Heigh-ho. I'll not speak a word more for a king's ransom.

FAUSTUS And what are you, Mistress Minx, the seventh and last?

LECHERY Who, I? I, sir? I am one that loves an inch of raw mutton better than an ell of fried stockfish, and the first letter of my name begins with lechery.

LUCIFER Away, to hell, away! On, piper!

Exeunt the Seven Sins

FAUSTUS O, how this sight doth delight my soul!

LUCIFER But Faustus, in hell is all manner of delight.

FAUSTUS O, might I see hell and return again safe, how happy were I then!

LUCIFER Faustus, thou shalt. At midnight I will send for thee. [*Presenting a book*] Meanwhile, peruse this book, and view it throughly, and thou shalt turn thyself into what shape thou wilt.

十顿饭和十次茶点——就这么一丁点儿，如何满足得了我的天性？我可是具有皇家血统的！我的父亲是一条腌猪腿，母亲是一大桶红葡萄酒。我的教父是腌鲱鱼彼得和牛肉马丁。我的教母，哟，那可是一个大家闺秀：大名是玛格丽三月啤酒小姐。浮士德，我的家世你都听见了，该邀请我吃晚饭了吧？

浮士德 我不邀请你。

饕餮 愿魔鬼掐死你！

浮士德 掐死你自己吧，饕餮！——你是谁，第六位？

懒惰 嗨嗬。我是懒惰。我出生在有阳光的沙滩上。嗨嗬。即便给我一座金山，我也懒得跟你再说一句话了。

浮士德 轻佻的夫人，你是谁？第七位，最后一位？

淫荡 你问我么，先生？我最爱的是那几两生羊肉，即便给我几斤炸鳕鱼，我也舍不得换。我的名字以"淫"开头。

撒旦 去，都给我回到地狱去！奏乐！

　　　七大罪孽下

浮士德 啊，这场景真让我心旷神怡！

撒旦 浮士德，地狱里有的是各种各样的快乐。

浮士德 如果能让我游览一次地狱，然后平安返回，那时我才高兴呢。

撒旦 浮士德，你可以去游览。半夜时我派人来叫你。[递过一本书]这本书你认真读读，到时候你自己就能随心所欲变形了。

FAUSTUS   [*Taking a book*] Thanks, mighty Lucifer! This will I keep as
    chary as my life.

LUCIFER   Now, Faustus, farewell.

FAUSTUS   Farewell, great Lucifer. Come, Mephistopheles.

    Exeunt, several ways

浮士德 ［接过书］谢谢你,伟大的魔王。我会
珍惜它如同生命的。

撒旦 再见,浮士德。

浮士德 再见,伟大的魔王。来吧,靡菲斯特。

分头下

ACT 3

第三幕

Enter the Chorus

CHORUS   Learned Faustus,

To know the secrets of astronomy

Graven in the book of Jove's high firmament,

Did mount him up to scale Olympus' top,

Where, sitting in a chariot burning bright,

Drawn by the strength of yoked dragons' necks,

He views the clouds, the planet and the stars,

The tropics, zones and quarters of the sky,

From the bright circle of the horned moon

Even to the height of *Primum Mobile*;

And, whirling round with this circumference

Within the concave compass of the pole,

From east to west his dragons swiftly glide

And in eight days did bring him home again.

Not long he stayed within his quiet house

Not long he stayed within his weary toil,

But now exploits do hale him out again,

And, mounted then upon a dragon's back,

解说员上

解说员　乔武的苍旻是一部巨著,

上面镌刻着宇宙的奥秘,

博学的浮士德追本穷源,

乘坐火焰四射的飞龙战车,

登上了奥林匹斯的山顶;

他观看云彩、行星、恒星、

回归线、地带和天的分层,

他的目光所及,从弯月的

圆周直达最高天的顶端,

他的龙车沿着轴干的凹面

就在这圆周体的上方盘旋,

从东往西,迅疾地滑行了

八个昼夜才返回他的家园。

这次疲惫的旅行过了不久,

他在宁静的住所已待不住,

新的冒险促使他再次出行:

他直接跨上了飞龙的背脊,

龙翼带他进入茫茫的天体。

That with his wings did part the subtle air,
He now is gone to prove cosmography,
And, as I guess, will first arrive at Rome,
To see the pope and manner of his court,
And take some part of holy Peter's feast,
That to this day is highly solemnized.

    Exit

这回他想验证宇宙的结构，
凌空观看海岸线和诸多王国。
我猜想，他首先会去罗马城
参见教皇，再看看教廷盛况，
然后分享神圣的圣彼得宴席，
那可是当今最隆重的典仪。

　　下

SCENE 1

Enter Faustus and Mephistopheles

FAUSTUS Having now, my good Mephistopheles,

Passed with delight the stately town of Trier

Environed round with airy mountaintops,

With walls of flint, and deep intrenched lakes,

Not to be won by any conquering prince;

From Paris next, coasting the realm of France,

We saw the river Maine fall into Rhine,

Whose banks are set with groves of fruitful vines;

Then up to Naples, rich Campania,

Whose buildings fair and gorgeous to the eye,

The streets straight forth, and paved with finest brick.

There saw we learned Maro's golden tomb,

The way he cut an English mile in length

Through a rock of stone in one night's space.

From thence to Venice, Padua, and the east,

In one of which a sumptuous temple stands,

That threats the stars with her aspiring top.

Whose frame is paved with sundry coloured stones,

90

第一场

浮士德、靡非斯特上

浮士德　好靡非斯特,你我快活逍遥,

游历了美丽的特里尔城[25],

那里四周都是崇山峻岭,

城墙固若金汤,湖泊深浚,

从不受域外霸主的侵凌。

然后我们经巴黎,涉法兰西沿海,

目睹了曼恩河注入莱茵湾,

河两岸的葡萄林果实累累。

那不勒斯和富饶的坎帕尼亚[26],

那里的建筑美不胜收,

笔直的街道全用砖石铺就。

那里我们拜谒过马罗[27]的金陵,

那条长达一英里的通道穿越

岩壁,被他一夜之间凿成。

我们还到过威尼斯和帕多瓦,

那里有座神庙极其雄伟壮丽,

它的外部全用各种彩石砌成,

仰之弥高的尖顶装饰得一片

And roofed aloft with curious work in gold.

Thus hitherto hath Faustus spent his time.

But tell me now what resting-place is this?

Hast thou, as erst I did command,

Conducted me within the walls of Rome?

MEPHISTOPHELES I have, my Faustus, and for proof thereof

This is the goodly palace of the pope;

And 'cause we are no common guests

I chose his privy chamber for our use.

FAUSTUS I hope his holiness will bid us welcome.

MEPHISTOPHELES All's one, for we'll be bold with his venison.

But now, my Faustus, that thou mayst perceive

What Rome contains for to delight thine eyes,

Know that this city stands upon seven hills

That underprop the groundwork of the same.

Just through the midst runs flowing Tiber's stream,

With winding banks that cut it in two parts,

Over the which two stately bridges lean,

That make safe passage to each part of Rome.

Upon the bridge called Ponte Angelo

Erected is a castle passing strong,

Where thou shalt see such store of ordinance

As that the double cannons, forged of brass,

Do match the number of days contained

Within the compass of one complete year—

金光闪耀,直刺高悬的星星。

浮士德就这样度过他的时光。

告诉我,这里又是什么地方?

你是否按照我事先的吩咐

带领我进入罗马的城门?

靡非斯特　我的浮士德,我已遵命而行,

这里就是教皇漂亮的宫廷。

由于我们不是普通的宾客,

我选择他的内室作为专用。

浮士德　希望教皇陛下欢迎我们到来。

靡非斯特　这倒无所谓,只要酒肉吃够就行。

我的浮士德,你过会就知道

罗马城有什么悦目的景观。

告诉你,这城建在七座山上,

山体支撑起地上的一切。

台伯河就从市中心流过,

弯曲的河岸把城市隔成两半,

河上架有两座雄伟的大桥,

方便两岸的居民安全通行。

那座叫安哲罗大桥的上方,

矗立着一座坚固的堡垒,

那里藏有许多法规条令,

还有双口径的铜制火炮,

它的数量正好与一年以内

太阳在黄道运行的天数相等。

Besides the gates, and high pyramides,

That Julius Caesar brought from Africa.

FAUSTUS　Now, by the kingdoms of infernal rule,

Of Styx, of Acheron, and the fiery lake

Of ever-burning Phlegethon, I swear

That I do long to see the monuments

And situation of bright splendent Rome.

Come, therefore, let's away!

MEPHISTOPHELES　Nay stay, my Faustus. I know you'd f see the pope

And take some part of holy Peter's feast,

The which this day with high solemnity

This day is held through Rome and Italy

In honour of the pope's triumphant victory.

FAUSTUS　Sweet Mephistopheles, thou pleasest me.

Whilst I am here on earth, let me be cloyed

With all things that delight the heart of man.

My four-and-twenty years of liberty

I'll spend in pleasure and in dalliance

That Faustus' name, whilst this bright frame doth stand,

May be admired through the furthest land.

MEPHISTOPHELES　'Tis well said, Faustus. Come, then, stand by me,

And thou shalt see them come immediately.

FAUSTUS　Nay, stay, my gentle Mephistopheles,

And grant me my request, and then I go.

Thou know'st within the compass of eight days

还有城门和尖塔也值得观瞻，

那是恺撒从非洲运回的战利品。

浮士德 好了，就凭魔鬼居住的王国，

凭冥河，凭地狱，凭烈火熊熊的

地狱火湖，我要在此发誓：

灿烂辉煌的罗马，它的名胜古迹、

山川河流，我一定要看看！

走吧走吧，我们这就动身！

靡非斯特 别急，浮士德，你不是想见教皇，

分享他神圣的彼得盛宴吗？

今天，就今天，为庆祝教皇的

丰功伟绩，全罗马城，全意大利，

都在举行这无比庄严的宴会。

浮士德 亲爱的靡非斯特，你真让我开心。

只要我活在世上一天，就让我

饱尝一切能愉悦人生的甘甜。

在这自由自在的二十四年中，

我要过得快活，尽情行欢作乐，

只要我堂堂的仪表尚在人世，

普天下人都仰慕浮士德这名字。

靡非斯特 说得好，浮士德，跟我站一块，

教廷中的人很快就过来。

浮士德 等一下，我温和的靡非斯特，

我还有一个请求，需要你答应：

你知道，在过去的八天里，

We viewed the face of heaven, of earth and hell.

So high our dragons soared into the air

That, looking down, the earth appeared to me

No bigger than my hand in quantity.

There did we view the kingdoms of the world,

And what might please mine eye I there beheld.

Then in this show let me an actor be,

That this proud pope my Faustus' cunning see.

MEPHISTOPHELES   Let is be so, my Faustus. But first stay

And view their triumphs as they pass this way,

And then devise what best contents thy mind,

By cunning in thine art, to cross the pope

Or dash the pride of this solemnity—

To make his monks and abbots stand like apes

And point like antics at his triple crown,

To beat the beads about the friar's pates

Or clap huge horns upon the cardinals' heads,

Or any villiany thou canst devise,

And I'll perform it, my Faustus. Hark, they come.

This day shall make thee be admired in Rome.

> *[They stand aside.] Enter the Cardinals [of France and Pa*
> *dua] and Bishops [of Lorraine and Rheims], some bearing*
> *crosiers, some the pillars; Monks and Friars singing their*
> *procession. Then the Pope [Adrian] and Raymond, King of*
> *Hungary, with Bruno [the rival Pope] led in chains. [The papal*

我们见过苍天、大地和地狱。

我们的飞龙高高升入太空，

往下看时，地球变得渺小至极，

论大小超不过我的一个巴掌。

我们在高空俯瞰地上的王国，

所见的景象真让我赏心悦目。

在下面的表演中，我要做个演员，

让高傲的教皇领教浮士德的手段。

靡非斯特　这没问题，浮士德。但不必操之过急，

你得先看看他们如何趾高气扬

走过这里，然后再使出你的手段，

按你的心愿痛快地激怒教皇，

消解这场聚会的隆重与庄严——

让他的僧侣和教士变成傻猴，

像一群小丑议论着他的三重冠。

让他们拿念珠敲托钵修士的脑袋，

用手拍打红衣主教头上的大角。

任何恶作剧你都可以导演，

由我付诸实施。注意，他们来了。

今天的你将被全罗马的人羡慕。

　　　　[他们退过一边。][法兰西]红衣主教、[帕多
　　　　瓦红衣主教、洛林主教、兰斯]主教上。众僧侣
　　　　和修道士唱着颂歌随后。再后是教皇[阿德里
　　　　安]、匈牙利国王雷蒙德和被缚的[伪教皇]布
　　　　鲁诺。[教皇的御座和布鲁诺的冠冕被人抬着

throne and Bruno's crown are borne in]

POPE   Cast down our footstool.

RAYMOND   Saxon Bruno, stoop,

> Whilst on thy back his holiness ascends
>
> Saint Peter's chair and state pontifical.

BRUNO   Proud Lucifer, that state belongs to me!

> But thus I fall to Peter, not to thee.

[He kneels in front of the throne]

POPE   To me and Peter shalt thou grovelling lie

> And crouch before the papal dignity.
>
> Sound trumpets, then, for thus Saint Peter's heir
>
> From Bruno's back ascends Saint Peter's chair.

A flourish while he ascends

> Thus, as the gods creep won with feet of wool
>
> Long ere with iron hands they punish men
>
> So shall our sleeping vengeance now arise
>
> And smite with death thy hated enterprise
>
> Lord Cardinals of France and Padua,
>
> Go forthwith to our holy consistory
>
> And read amongst the statutes decretal
>
> What, by the holy council held at Trent,
>
> The sacred synod hat decreed for him
>
> That doth assume the papal government
>
> Without election and a true consent.
>
> Away, and bring us word with speed.

殿后]

教皇 放下脚凳。

雷蒙德 撒克逊的布鲁诺,跪下!

圣彼得的御座、庄严的法衣、

教皇的神圣,要从你的背上升起。

布鲁诺 骄傲的魔鬼,这荣耀属于我!

我可以向彼得下跪,不是向你们。

[布鲁诺在教皇御座前下跪]

教皇 你得向我和彼得卑躬屈节,

面对教皇的尊严,你得蹲伏。

喇叭吹起来! 圣彼得的继承人

脚踩布鲁诺,登上圣彼得宝座。

喇叭奏花腔。阿德里安踏布鲁诺背脊登上御座

天神的行踪向来悄然无声,

他们用铁腕惩治人类的罪行,

我们沉睡的复仇神也已苏醒,

他发出致命一击,惩治你的野心。

法兰西和帕多瓦的两位红衣主教,

你俩赶紧去一趟神圣评议会,

查阅一下教皇颁布的法规条文:

当年在特伦特召开的神学会议

曾制订过怎样的条例惩治违教者,

即那些未经选举、未获神许、

僭越教皇的权威的不法之徒。

快去,我们等你们的消息。

FIRSRT CARDINAL We go, my lord.

Exeunt Cardinals

POPE Lord Raymond—

[*Pope Adrian and Raymond converse apart*]

FAUSTUS [*aside*] Go haste thee, gentle Mephistopheles

Follow the cardinals to the consistory,

And as they turn their superstitious books

Strike them with sloth and drowsy idleness,

And make them sleep so sound that in their shapes

Thyself and I may parley with this pope,

This proud confronter of the emperor,

And in despite of all his holiness

Restore this Bruno to his liberty

And bear him to the states of Germany.

MEPHISTOPHELES Faustus, I go.

FAUSTUS Dispatch it soon.

The pope shall curse that Faustus came to Rome.

Exeunt Faustus and Mephistopheles

BRUNO Pope Adrian, let me have some right of law.

I was elected by the emperor.

POPE We will depose the emperor for that deed

And curse the people that submit to him.

Both he and thou shalt stand excommunicate

And interdict from Church's privilege

And all society of holy men.

法兰西红衣主教 我们这就去,教皇阁下。

法兰西红衣主教、帕多瓦红衣主教下

教皇 雷蒙德大人——

[教皇与雷蒙德退至一旁交谈]

浮士德 快去,温和的靡非斯特,

跟上红衣主教,去评议会看看,

当他们查阅那些迷信书籍时,

你就念起懒惰和昏迷的咒语,

让他们呼呼入睡;这时你和我

就可扮成他们模样与教皇交谈。

这傲慢的家伙跟德国皇帝作对,

我们无须顾及他如何的神圣,

先恢复这位布鲁诺的自由,

把他弄回到德国的王宫。

靡非斯特 浮士德,我这就去。

浮士德 速速办理!

我要让教皇诅咒浮士德来到罗马。

浮士德、靡非斯特下

布鲁诺 阿德里安教皇,你得依法处置我,

我这教皇是德国皇帝遴选出来的。

教皇 为此我要废黜这个皇帝,

诅咒所有臣服于他的百姓。

我要开除你们两人的教籍,

剥夺你们在教会所享的权利,

不许你们参加任何神圣团体。

He grows too proud in his authority,

Lifting his lofty head above the clouds,

And like a steeple overpeers the Church.

But we'll pull down his haughty insolence.

And as Pope Alexander, our progenitor,

Trod on the neck of German Frederick,

Adding this golden sentence to our praise,

'That Peter's heirs should tread on emperors

And walk upon the dreadful adder's back,

Treading the lion and the dragon down,

And fearless spurn the killing basilisk',

So will we quell that haughty schismatic

And by authority apostolical

Depose him from his regal government.

BRUNO   Pope Julius swore to princely Sigismond,

For him and the succeeding popes of Rome,

To hold the emperors their lawful lords.

POPE   Pope Julius abuse the Church's rights,

And therefore none of his decrees can stand.

Is not all power on earth bestowed on us?

And therefore, though we would, we cannot err.

Behold this silver belt, whereto is fixed

Seven golden keys fast sealed with seven seals

In token of our sevenfold power from heaven,

To bind or loose, lock fast, condemn, or judge,

他大权在握,太专横跋扈了,

他已经将脑袋升入云霄之上,

就像塔尖俯视下面的教堂。

我要灭了他不可一世的傲气,

就像前辈亚历山大教皇那样

把脚踩在腓特烈皇帝[28]的脖子上,

并在我们的祷词中添一金律:

"彼得的继承人脚踩帝王,

行走在可恶的毒蛇的背上,

狮子和毒龙都倒毙在他脚下,

害人的蛇怪难逃无畏的一踹。"

我们要剪除不可一世的分裂者,

凭使徒代代相传的权威,

把他从王权的宝座上废黜。

布鲁诺　朱利斯教皇对高贵的西吉斯孟发过誓:

他和他以后的所有罗马教皇

将视皇帝为他们合法的君主。[29]

教皇　朱利斯教皇滥用教会的权力,

他所颁布的法令不能算数。

人间的权力都归我们掌管,

我们即便存心,也不可能犯错。

看看这条银带子,上面挂着

七把金钥匙,还有七枚印玺,

象征着上天赋予的七重权力:

捆绑或松绑、关押、判刑或定罪,

Resign, or seal, or whatso pleaseth us.

Then he and thou and all the world should stoop,

Or be assured of our dreadful curse

To light as heavy as the pains of hell.

Enter Faustus and Mephistopheles, [dressed] like the cardinals

MEPHISTOPHELES [*aside to Faustus*]

Now to tell, Faustus, are we not fitted well?

FAUSTUS [*aside to Mephistopheles*]

Yes, Mephistopheles, and two such cardinals

Ne'er served a holy pope as we shall do.

But whilst they sleep within the consistory,

Let us salute his reverend fatherhood.

RAYMOND [*to the Pope*]

Behold, my lord, the cardinals are returned.

POPE Welcome, grave fathers. Answer presently:

What have our holy council there decreed

Concerning Bruno and the emperor

In quittance of their late conspiracy

Against our state and papal dignity?

FAUSTUS Most sacred patron of the Church of Rome,

By full consent of all the synod

Of priests and prelates, it is thus decreed:

That Bruno and the Germany emperor

Be held as Lollards and bold schismatcis

And proud disturber of the Church's pease.

签署或拒签,一切看我们高兴。

不光你和他,整个世界都得下跪,

我们可怕的诅咒不容人置疑,

它降下的痛苦不啻万恶的地狱。

　　　　　浮士德和靡非斯特化身红衣主教上

靡非斯特　[对浮士德]

浮士德,你看我们打扮得还好吧。

浮士德　[对靡非斯特]

很好,靡非斯特,说到为教皇服务,

那两个红衣主教一定不如我们称职。

趁他们在评议会大楼呼呼大睡,

我们这就去拜见可敬的神父。

雷蒙德　[对教皇]

看,阁下,红衣主教回来了。

教皇　欢迎,严明的教父,快说说,

我们神圣的评议会颁布了

怎样的条例,适合用来惩处

布鲁诺和德皇最近的阴谋,

他俩胆大包天,冒犯教皇尊严。

浮士德　罗马教会最神圣的庇护人,

经僧侣团和高级教士会议

一致通过的该决议是这样的:

布鲁诺和德国皇帝是公认的

罗拉德派信徒,无耻的分立论者,

破坏教会和平的狂妄之徒。

And if that Bruno by his own assent,

Without enforcement of the German peers,

Did seek to wear the triple diadem

And by your death to climb Saint Peter's chair,

The statutes decretal have thus decreed:

He shall be straight condemned of heresy

And on a pile of faggots burnt to death.

POPE It is enough. Here, take him to your charge,

And bear him straight to Ponte Angelo,

And in the strongest tower enclose him fast.

Tomorrow, sitting in our consistory

With all our college of grave cardinals

We will determine of his life or death.

Here, take his triple crown along with you

And leave it in the Church's treasury.

[*Bruno's papal crown is given to Faustus and Mephistopheles*]

Make haste again, mu good lord cardinals,

And take our blessing apostolical.

MEPHISTOPHELES [*aside*]

So, so, was never devil thus blessed before!

FAUSTUS [*aside*] Away, sweet Mephistopheles, begone.

The cardinals will be plagued for this anon.

Exeunt Faustus and Mephistopheles [with Bruno]

POPE Go presently and bring a banquet forth,

That we may solemnize Saint Peter's feast

布鲁诺本人更是自作主张，

未经德国王公贵族的劝进

便图谋戴上教皇的三重冠，

欲登彼得之位，取代阁下。

罗马教廷对他的裁决是：

以传播左道邪说罪论处，

堆起柴火，把此人烧死。

教皇　这就好了。我把他交给你们，

马上将他押到安哲罗堡垒，

找一间最坚固的牢房关起来。

明天，我们的宗教法庭开庭，

红衣主教团全体成员出席，

我们要决定布鲁诺的生死。

他的三重冠你们也带过去，

由教会的金库收藏。

　　　［教皇将布鲁诺的王冠交给浮士德和靡非斯特］

快去吧，两位好主教阁下，

使徒相传的神恩眷顾你们！

靡非斯特　［旁白］

魔鬼获神恩眷顾，倒真新鲜！

浮士德　［旁白］走吧走吧，好靡非斯特，

红衣主教很快要遭瘟了。

　　　浮士德、靡非斯特［带布鲁诺］下

教皇　大家快去，把宴席布置起来，

圣彼得宴会要办得庄严隆重，

107

And with Lord Raymond, king of Hungary,
Drink to our late and happy victory.

Exeunt

我们要与匈牙利国王雷蒙德
一起干杯,庆祝最近的胜利!

　　同下

SCENE 2

A sennet while the banquet is brought in. [Seats are provided at the banquet. Exeunt Attendants,] and then enter Faustus and Mephistopheles in their own shapes

MEPHISTOPHELES   Now, Faustus, come, prepare thyself for mirth.

The sleepy cardinals are hard at hand

To censure Bruno, that is posted hence

And on a proud-paced steed, as swift as thought,

Flies o'er the Alps to fruitful Germany,

There to salute the woeful emperor.

FAUSTUS   The pope will curse them for their sloth today,

That slept both Bruno and his clown away.

But now, that Faustus may delight his mind

And by their folly make some merriment,

Sweet Mephistopheles, so charm me here

That I may walk invisible to all

And do whate'er I please, unseen of any.

MEPHISTOPHELES   Faustus, thou shalt. Then kneel down presently,

   [Faustus kneels]

Whilst on thy head I lay my hand

第二场

喇叭响起,奏乐的同时,众仆役布置宴席。[座位
摆放好后,众仆役退下。]接着浮士德与靡非斯
特以本来面目上

靡非斯特　浮士德,你现在可以快活逍遥了。

沉沉入睡的红衣主教鞭长莫及

再不能训斥布鲁诺。他一到这里,

便骑上神骏,快马加鞭越过

阿尔卑斯山,前往富庶的德国,

去致意那位愁眉苦脸的皇帝。

浮士德　这一觉睡掉了布鲁诺和他的王冠,

教皇一定大发雷霆,诅咒他们的懒散。

现在的浮士德已经喜上眉梢,

存心要拿他们的愚蠢取笑。

亲爱的靡非斯特,你给我念个咒,

我要隐去凡躯,不为人所见,

随心所欲做我想做的事情。

靡非斯特　浮士德,我马上照办。请蹲下身子。

[浮士德蹲下]

我这只手就在你的头上,

And charm thee with this magic wand.

[Presenting a magic girdle]

First wear this girdle, then appear

Invisible to all are here.

The planets seven, the gloomy air,

Hell, and the Furies' forked hair,

Pluto's blue fire, and Hecate's tree

With magic spells so compass thee

That no eye may thy body see.

[Faustus rises]

So, Faustus, now, for all their holiness,

Do what thou wilt, thou shalt not be discerned.

FAUSTUS   Thanks, Mephistopheles. Now, friars, take heed

Lest Faustus make your shaven crowns to bleed.

MEPHISTOPHELES   Faustus, no more. See where the cardinals come.

Enter Pope and all the lords: [Raymond, King of Hungary, the Archbishop of Rheims, etc., Friars and Attendants.] enter the [two] Cardinals [of France and Padua] with a book

POPE   Welcome, lord cardinals. Come, sit down.

Lord Raymond, take your seat.

[They sit]

Friars, attend,

And see that all things be in readiness,

As best beseems this solemn festivals.

FIRST CARDINAL   First, may it please your sacred holiness

这根魔杖威力非凡。

[递过一根魔带]

只要你系上这根带子,

就不会有人看见你。

七大行星,阴沉沉的天,

黑暗的地狱,头发分叉的复仇女神,

冥王普鲁托的硫黄火,赫卡忒的绞刑架,

都以魔咒环绕你,促使

肉眼见不着你的躯体。

[浮士德起身]

浮士德,凭这一切的神性,

随意而为吧,没人看见你了。

浮士德　多谢了,靡非斯特。教士们,留神点!

小心浮士德打破你们的秃头。

靡非斯特　浮士德,嘘——,他们来了。

教皇偕匈牙利国王雷蒙德、兰斯大主教、修道
士、侍从上。[法兰西、帕多瓦]红衣主教自另一
侧上,每人都携带一本书

教皇　欢迎,两位红衣主教。来,这边坐。

雷蒙德陛下,您请坐。

[众人就座]

各位修士,

你们负责把一切准备妥当,

这次宴会一定要办得隆重圆满。

法兰西红衣主教　神圣的教皇,可敬的宗教会议

To view the sentence of the reverend synod

Concerning Bruno and the emperor?

POPE   What needs this question? Did I not tell you

Tomorrow we would sit i'th'consistory

And there determine of his punishment?

You brought us word even now, it was decreed

That Bruno and the cursed emperor

Were by the holy council both condemned

For loathed Lollards and base schismatics

Then wherefore would you have me view this book?

FIRST CARDINAL   Your grace mistakes. You gave us no such charge.

RAYMOND   Deny it not. We all are witnessed

That Bruno here was late delivered you,

With his rich triple crown to be reserved

And put into the Church's treasury.

BOTH CARDINALS   By holy Paul, we saw them not.

POPE   By Peter, you shall die

Unless you bring them forth immediately.—

Hale them to prison. Lade their limbs with gyves!—

False prelates, for this hateful treachery

Curst be your souls to hellish misery.

> *[Exeunt Attendants with the two Cardinals]*

FAUSTUS   *[aside]*

So, they are safe. Now, Faustus, to the feast.

The pope had never such a frolic guest.

就布鲁诺和皇帝制订的条例,

您是否可以先让大家看看?

教皇 你问的是什么呀?我不是告诉过你

明天我们就要召开宗教大会,

会上将决定如何惩罚这两人吗?

刚才你不是还跟我们说过:

按照神圣的会议所颁布的法规,

布鲁诺和那位皇帝应受严惩,

因为他们是卑鄙的罗拉德派和分立论者,

你怎么还让我出示处罚条例呢?

法兰西红衣主教 陛下弄错了。我们没说过那样的话。

雷蒙德 别否认了。我们大家都可见证,

教皇把布鲁诺交给了你们两人,

他那顶漂亮的三重冠,也由你们

负责送进教会的金库保存。

两位红衣主教 圣保罗做证,我们什么也没见过。

教皇 圣彼得在上,你们得处死,

除非马上把人和三重冠交出来——

拉下去,关进监狱!手和脚都铐起来。

伪善的教士,凭这可恨的叛逆行为,

得把你们的灵魂打入地狱的深渊。

     [侍从押红衣主教下]

浮士德 [旁白]

这两位打发掉了。现在去赴宴。

如此爱热闹的客人,教皇一定见所未见。

115

POPE Lord Archbishop of Rheims, sit down with us.

ARCHBISHOP [*sitting*] I thank your holiness.

FAUSTUS Fall to. The devil choke you an you spare!

POPE Who's that spoke? Friars, look about.

    [*Some Friars attempt to search*]

    Lord Raymond, prey fall to. I am beholding

    To the bishop of Milan for this so rare a present.

FAUSTUS [*snatching the meat*] I thank you, sir.

POPE How now! Who snatched the meat from me?

    Villains, why speak you not? —

    My good lord Lord Archbishop, here's a most dainty dish

    Was sent me from a cardinal in France.

FAUSTUS [*snatching the dish*] I will have that, too.

POPE What Lollards do attend our holiness,

    That we receive such indignity?

    Fetch me some wine.

    [*Wine is brought*]

FAUSTUS [*aside*] Ay, pray do, for Faustus is adry.

POPE Lord Raymond, I drink unto your grace.

FAUSTUS [*snatching the cup*] I pledge your grace.

POPE My wine gone, too? Ye lubbers, look about

    And find the man that doth this villainy,

    Or by our sanctitude you all shall die! —

    [*Some Friars search out*]

    I pray, my lords, have patience at this troublesome banquet.

教皇　兰斯大主教,我们入席吧。

兰斯大主教　[坐下]谢谢陛下。

浮士德　吃吧。魔鬼噎死你们这班讨厌的教士。

教皇　谁在说话?各位修士,你们看看。

　　　　[众修道士四下搜寻]

　　雷蒙德阁下,米兰主教送来的

　　这份贡品,真是稀有的美食佳肴。

浮士德　[抢过肉食]谢谢陛下。

教皇　怎么回事?谁抢走了我的肉?

　　混蛋,你们为什么不说话?——

　　我的大主教,这份精致的美食

　　是法兰西红衣主教进贡的。

浮士德　[抢过那道菜肴]这也给我吧。

教皇　我们神圣的聚宴,怎么会有

　　罗拉德派混进来?如此放肆!

　　给我来点酒。

　　　　[侍从斟酒]

浮士德　[旁白]快斟快斟,浮士德早已口渴难忍。

教皇　雷蒙德阁下,为您的健康干杯!

浮士德　[抢过银杯]让我来为阁下干杯。

教皇　我的酒也不见了?你们这班混蛋,

　　快找找,把这个恶棍给我揪出来,

　　否则,你们今天都别想活了!——

　　　　[几位修道士在室内搜寻]

　　真乱了套了,诸位,别慌!别慌!

ARCHBISHOP   Please it your holiness, I think it be some ghost crept out of

purgatory and now is come unto your holiness for his pardon.

POPE   It may be so.

Go, then ,command our priests to sing a dirge

To lay the fury of this same troublesome ghost.

[Exit one. The Pope crosses himself]

FAUSTUS   How now?   Must every bit be spiced with a cross?

[The Pope crosses himself]

Nay, then, take that!

[Faustus gives the Pope a blow on the head]

POPE   O, I am slain! Help me, my lords.

O, come and help to bear my body hence.

Damned be this soul for ever for this deed!

Exeunt the Pope and his train

MEPHISTOPHELES   Now, Faustus, what will you do now?   For I can tell

you you'll be cursed with bell, book and candle.

FAUSTUS   Bell, book, and candle; candle, book, and bell,

Forward and backward, to curse Faustus to hell.

Enter the Friars with bell, book, and candle, for the dirge

FIRST FRIAR   Come, brethren, let's about our business with good devotion.

[The Friars chant]

Cursed be he that stole away his holiness' meat from the table.

Maledicat Dominus!

Cursed be he that struck his holiness a blow on the face.

Maledicat Dominus!

118

大主教 陛下,一定是某个小鬼从炼狱逃出,

来这里恳求陛下赦免他的罪孽了。

教皇 有这可能。

去,吩咐教士们唱一首挽歌,

超度超度这个不安宁的鬼魂。

[一教士下。教皇在胸前画十字]

浮士德 怎么啦?用得着大事小事都画十字吗?

[教皇继续画十字]

好,让你画!

[浮士德一巴掌打在教皇脸上]

教皇 哎哟,杀人了!救命啊,诸位救我!

快来救我,快保护我离开这里。

居然敢打我,谁打我谁下地狱!

教皇与众教士逃下

靡非斯特 浮士德,下面你想干什么?告诉你,过一会他

们就会拿铃铛、经书和蜡烛来诅咒你了。

浮士德 经书、铃铛加蜡烛,蜡烛、铃铛加经书,

颠来倒去,无非是想让浮士德下地狱。

众教士持铃铛、经书和蜡烛上

教士甲 来吧,教友们,让我们恭敬地唱起来。

[众教士唱挽歌]

从教皇桌子上偷窃肉食的该受诅咒。

愿上帝惩罚他!

打了教皇一巴掌的该受诅咒。

愿上帝惩罚他!

Cursed be he that struck Friar Sandelo a blow on the pate.

Maledicat Dominus!

Cursed be he that disturbeth our holy dirge.

Maledicat Dominus!

Cursed be he that took away his holiness' wine.

Maledicat Dominus!

> [*Faustus and Mephistopheles*] *beat the Friars, and fling firework*[*s*] *among them, and exeunt*

打了桑德罗修士脑门的该受诅咒。

愿上帝惩罚他!

谁捣乱我们神圣的挽歌,谁受诅咒。

愿上帝惩罚他!

偷走了教皇银杯的该受诅咒。

愿上帝惩罚他!

　　[浮士德和靡非斯特]殴打众教士,朝他们掷烟
　　火。众教士逃走;浮士德和靡非斯特追下

SCENE 3

Enter Clown [Robin], and Dick with a cup

DICKB Sirrah Robin, we were best look that your devil can answer the stealing of this same cup, for the Vintner's boy follows us at the hard heels.

ROBIN 'Tis no matter. Let him come. An he follow us, I'll so conjure him as he was never conjured in his life, I warrant him. Let me see the cup.

Enter Vintner

DICK [*giving the cup to Robin*] Here 'tis. Yonder he comes. Now, Robin, now or never show thy cunning.

VINTNER O, are you here? I am glad I have found you. You are a couple of fine companions! Pray, where's the cup you stole from the tavern?

ROBIN How, how? We steal a cup? Take heed what you say. We look not like cup-stealers, I can tell you.

VINTNER Never deny' t, for I know you have it, and I'll search you.

ROBIN Search me? Ay, and spare not. [*Aside to Dick, tossing him the cup*] Hold the cup, Dick. [*To the Vintner*] Come, come, search me, search me.

第三场

小丑[罗宾]和迪克上。迪克持一银杯。

迪克　罗宾伙计,我们最好想想清楚,如何应对偷盗
　　这个银杯的指控,酒店老板的仆人正紧跟在我们
　　身后呢。

罗宾　没关系,让他来吧。如果他执意跟踪,我向你保证,
　　我会在他身上施行魔法,那是他这一辈子都没见过
　　的。让我看看这个杯子。

酒店老板上

迪克　[递银杯给罗宾]给。他过来了。罗宾,记住,别要你
　　的小聪明。

酒店老板　你们在这里啊?很高兴找到你们。你俩真是一
　　对好伙伴! 说吧,从酒店里偷来的银杯子藏到哪里去
　　了?

罗宾　你说什么? 我们偷银杯子? 注意你所说的话。
　　我们可不像偷杯子的那种人,我可以告诉你。

酒店老板　别否认了,我知道是你们偷的。我要搜搜你们。

罗宾　搜我吗? 是该搜搜。[向迪克挪近,把杯子塞给他]
　　收好杯子,迪克。[对酒店老板]来吧,来吧,搜搜我,
　　搜搜我。

123

[The Vintner searches Robin]

VINTNER   *[to Dick]* Come on, sirrah, let me search you now.

DICK   Ay, ay, do, do. *[Aside to Robin, tossing him the cup]* Hold the cup, Robin. *[To the Vintner]* I fear not your searching. We scorn to steal your cups, I can tell you.

[The Vintner searches Dick]

VINTNER   Never outface me for the matter, for sure the cup is between you two.

ROBIN   *[brandishing the cup]* Nay, there you lie. 'Tis beyond us both.

VINTNER   A plague take you! I thought 'twas your knavery to take it away. Come, give it me again.

ROBIN   Ay, much! When, can you tell? Dick, make me a circle, and stand close at my back, and stir not for thy life. *[Dick makes a circle]* Vintner, you shall have your cup anon. Say nothing, Dick. 'O' *per se* 'o', Demogorgon, Belcher, and Mephistopheles!

Enter Mephistopheles. [Exit the Vintner, running]

MEPHISTOPHELES   You princely legions of infernal rule,

How am I vexed by these villains' charms!

From Constantinople have they brought me now

Only for pleasure of these damned slaves.

ROBIN   By Lady, sir, you have had a shrewd journey of it. Will it please you to take a shoulder of mutton to supper and a tester in your purse, and go back again?

DICK   Ay, I pray you heartily, sir, for we called you but in jest, I promise you.

124

[酒店老板搜罗宾]

酒店老板 [对迪克]过来,伙计,我现在得搜搜你了。

迪克 好,好,搜吧,搜吧。[向罗宾挪近,把杯子塞给他] 收好杯子,罗宾。[对酒店老板]我可不怕你搜。我才 不屑于偷银杯子呢,我告诉你。

[酒店老板搜迪克]

酒店老板 别这样看着我,我敢肯定,杯子一定在你们两 人身上。

罗宾 [举起酒杯]你说谎。不可能在我们身上。

酒店老板 你俩真该死! 我知道,一定是你们耍把戏把杯 子藏起来了。唉,你们就还给我吧。

罗宾 好,好,马上还给你。迪克,给我画一个圈,然后一 动不动地站到我的背后。[迪克画了一个圈]店老板, 你马上就能找回杯子。别说话,迪克。[念咒召唤魔 鬼]"O"即为"O",狄摩高根,贝尔契,靡非斯特!

靡非斯特上。[酒店老板逃走]

靡非斯特 无比高贵的阴间精灵啊,

两个恶棍咒得我心神不定!

我从君士坦丁堡匆匆赶来,

原来只是被两奴才寻开心。

罗宾 圣母在上,先生,你这一趟来得真神速。麻烦你再 回去一次,背一大块羊肉来给我们当晚饭,另外再捎 上一口袋银币。

迪克 是的,先生,我答应你,会衷心为你祈祷,毕竟把你 召唤来是为了好玩。

MEPHISTOPHELES   To purge the rashness of this cursed deed,

First, [*To Dick*] be thou turned to this ugly shape,

For apish deeds transformed to an ape.

   [*Dick is transformed in shape*]

ROBIN   O brave, an ape! I pray, sir, let me have the carrying of him about to show some tricks.

MEPHISTOPHELES   And so thou shalt. Be thou transformed to a dog, and carry him upon thy back. Away, begone!

   [*Robin is transformed in shape*]

ROBIN   A dog? That's excellent. Let the maids look well to their porridge pots, for I'll into the kitchen presently. Come, Dick, come.

   Exeunt the two Clowns [*with Dick on Robin's back*]

MEPHISTOPHELES   Now with the flames of ever-burning fire

I'll wing myself and forthwith fly amain

Unto my Faustus, to the Great Turk's court.

   Exit

靡非斯特　如此鲁莽的恶作剧必须清算,

　　　[对迪克]首先,我得变变这个丑八怪:

　　你做了一件适合猴子做的事,

　　我就把你变成一只猴子吧。

　　　　[迪克变形,成了一只猴子]

罗宾　好哇,一只猴子! 先生,我求你,让我背上这只猴子

　　去表演马戏吧。

靡非斯特　可以。我要把你变成一只狗,让你把它扛在背

　　上。变! 滚吧!

　　　　[罗宾变形,成了一只狗]

罗宾　一只狗？太好了。让姑娘们留心看好自己的粥罐子

　　吧,我马上就要进厨房了。来吧,迪克,来吧。

　　　　[迪克骑罗宾背上,]两小丑下

靡非斯特　带着永远燃烧的地狱之火,我现在

　　要张开双翼,急急飞向浮士德,

　　然后再去雄伟的土耳其王宫。

　　　靡非斯特下

ACT 4

第四幕

SCENE 1

Enter Martino and Frederick at several doors

MARTINO   What ho, officers, gentlemen!

Hie to the presence to attend the emperor.

Good Frederick, see the rooms be voided straight;

His majesty is coming to the hall.

Go back, and see the state in readiness.

FREDERICK   But where is Bruno, our elected pope,

That on a Fury's back come post from Rome?

Will not his grace consort this emperor?

MARTINO   O, yes, and with him comes the German conjurer,

The learned Faustus, fame of Wittenberg,

The wonder of the world for magic art;

And he intends to show great Carolus

The race of all his stout progenitors,

And bring in presence of his majesty

The royal shapes and warlike semblances

Of Alexander and his beauteous paramour.

FREDERICK   Where is Benvolio?

MARTINO   Fast asleep, I warrant you.

第一场

马丁诺、弗雷德里克各自一门上

马丁诺　嗬,各位王公,各位乡绅,快去

晋见皇帝陛下! 好弗雷德里克,

由你负责把房间布置停当;

皇帝陛下马上要到大厅来。

你们回去,把宝座准备起来。

弗雷德里克　我们自己选出的教皇布鲁诺

乘坐复仇神的羽翼从罗马回返,

他如今何在? 是否也来陪伴皇帝陛下?

马丁诺　是的,与他同来的还有德国魔法师,

那位博学的浮士德,维腾堡的名人,

论魔法艺术堪称世界的奇迹。

浮士德有意施法,为理查大帝

显现他神武皇族的列祖列宗;

他还要当着皇帝的面,召唤

高贵而勇武的亚历山大的附体

以及他那位美艳超绝的情人。

弗雷德里克　班佛里奥在哪里?

马丁诺　我向你保证,他一定在呼呼大睡。

131

He took his rouse with stoups of Rhenish wine

So kindly yesternight to Bruno's health

That all this day the sluggard keeps his bed.

FREDERICK   See, see, his window's ope. We'll call to him.

MARTINO   What ho, Benvolio!

Enter Benvolio above a window, in his nightcap, buttoning

BENVOLIO   What a decil ail you two?

MARTINO   Speak softly, sir, lest the devil hear you;

For Faustus at the court is late arrived,

And at his heels a thousand Furies wait

To accomplish whatsoever the doctor please.

BENVOLIO   What of this?

MARTINO   Come, leave the chamber first, and thou shalt see

This conjurer perform such rare exploits

Before the pope and the royal emperor

As never yet was seen in Germany.

BENVOLIO   Has not the pope enough of conjuring yet?

He was upon the devil's back late enough;

And if he be so far in love with him,

I would he would post with him to Rome again.

FREDERICK   Speak, wilt thou come and see this sport?

BENVOLIO   Not I.

MARTINO   Wilt thou stand in thy window and see it, then?

BENVOLIO   Ay, an I fall not asleep i' th' meantime.

MARTINO   The emperor is at hand, who comes to see

昨天晚上，为祝布鲁诺的健康，

他豪饮莱茵河水酿制的葡萄酒，

这下只能懒汉般整天横卧床上了。

弗雷德里克　看，他的门窗打开了。我们去叫他。

马丁诺　喂喂，班佛里奥！

　　　　　　班佛里奥从上方窗口现身，头戴睡帽，扣紧衣扣子

班佛里奥　两人见什么鬼啊？

马丁诺　说话轻点，担心被魔鬼听见；

浮士德刚刚来到我们的宫廷，

侍候他的鬼怪成百上千，

只要他高兴，什么事都能办成。

班佛里奥　那又怎么样？

马丁诺　你快下来吧，过会你就能领教

魔法大师在教皇和皇帝面前

如何将无与伦比的魔法表演，

那一定为全德国闻所未闻。

班佛里奥　他的魔法教皇还没领教够吗？

最近魔鬼把他背到这里的次数够多了；

如果魔鬼真的那么爱他，

我愿魔鬼即刻送他回罗马。

弗雷德里克　说吧，你到底要不要看这场表演？

班佛里奥　我不要看。

马丁诺　你准备在自己的窗口看，是不是？

班佛里奥　是的，只要到时候我不睡着。

马丁诺　皇帝就要到了，他这次前来

What wonders by black spells may compassed be.

BENVOLIO   Well, go you attend the emperor. I am content for once to thrust my head out at a window, for they say if a man be drunk overnight the devil cannot turn him in the morning. If that be true, I have a charm in my head shall control him as well as the conjurer, I warrant you.

> *Exeunt* [*Frederick and Martino. Benvolio remains at his window.*]
> *A sennet.* [*Enter*] *Charles the German Emperor, Bruno,* [*the Duke of*] *Saxony, Faustus, Mephistopheles, Frederick, Martino, and Attendants.* [*The Emperor sits in his throne*]

EMPEROR   Wonder of men, renowned magician,

Thrice-learned Faustus, welcome to our court.

This deed of thine, in setting Bruno free

From his and our professed enemy,

Shall add more excellence unto thine art

Than if be powerful necromantic spells

Thou couldst command the world's obedience.

For ever be beloved of Carolus.

And if this Bruno thou hast late redeemed

In peace possess the triple diadem

And sit in Peter's chair, despite of chance,

Thou shalt be famous through Italy

And honoured of the German emperor.

FAUSTUS   These gracious words, most royal Carolus,

Shall make poor Faustus to his utmost power

134

就为观看魔咒如何创造奇迹。

班佛里奥　好吧,你们侍候皇帝去吧。至于我,能够在窗
　　　口前伸伸脖子,我就很满足了。古话说得好:晚上喝
　　　醉酒,凌晨的魔鬼躲着走。如果这话是真的,那我脑
　　　子里一定藏着咒语,足以控制魔鬼,就像魔法师那
　　　样,我可以向你保证。

　　　　[弗雷德里克、马丁诺]下。[班佛里奥仍留在窗
　　　　口前。]喇叭奏花腔。德国皇帝理查、布鲁诺、萨
　　　　克森[公爵]、浮士德、靡非斯特、弗雷德里克、马
　　　　丁诺、若干侍从[上]。[皇帝坐上宝座]

皇帝　人类的奇迹,闻名天下的魔法师,

　　　博学的浮士德,欢迎你来到

　　　我们的宫廷! 你把布鲁诺从

　　　我们共同的敌人手中解救出来,

　　　这一壮举为你的法术争得光荣,

　　　不亚于你利用威力强大的魔咒

　　　玩弄整个世界于你的股掌。

　　　我理查本人永远敬你爱你。

　　　如果被你救下的这位布鲁诺

　　　平平安安戴上三重冠,不管

　　　局势如何,都能登上彼得宝座,

　　　那时你的名声一定传遍意大利,

　　　德国皇帝我也一定加倍崇敬你。

浮士德　无比高贵的皇帝陛下,您的美言

　　　足以让贫贱的浮士德肝脑涂地

Both love and serve the German emperor

And lay his life at holy Bruno's feet.

For proof whereof, if so your grace be pleased,

The doctor stands prepared by power of art

To cast his magic charms, that shall pierce through

The ebon gates of ever-burning hell

And hale the stubborn Furies from their caves

To compass whatsoe'er your grace commands.

BENVOLIO [*aside, at the window*] Blood, he speaks terribly. But for all that, I do not greatly believe him. He looks as like a conjurer as the pope to a costermonger.

EMPEROR Then, Faustus, as thou late didst promise us,

We would behold that famous conqueror

Great Alexander and his paramour

In their true shapes and state majestical,

That we may wonder at their excellence.

FAUSTUS Your majesty shall see them presently.—

[*Aside to Mephistopheles*] Mephistopheles, away,

And with a solemn noise of trumpet's sound

Present before this royal emperor

Great Alexander and his beauteous paramour.

MEPHISTOPHELES [*aside to Faustus*] Faustus, I will.

[*Exit Mephistopheles*]

BENVOLIO [*at the window*] Well, Master Doctor, an your devils come not away quickly, you shall have me asleep presently. Zounds, I

敬爱陛下,为陛下效犬马之劳,

并终身追随神圣的布鲁诺。

作为见证,本博士已准备妥当,

只要陛下高兴,他将凭魔法神威,

念动咒语,直捣永远燃烧的

地狱的门,将从洞穴招来

脾气古怪的复仇女神,让她们

如实履行皇帝陛下的号令。

班佛里奥　［在窗口旁白］我的天,说得真好听。但我无论

如何不相信他的鬼话。如果他是魔法师,那菜贩子就

是教皇了。

皇帝　浮士德,请履行刚才许下的诺言,

我们想亲眼看看那位著名的征服者

亚历山大大帝和他漂亮的情人。

我们对他的丰功伟绩特别好奇,

请你施法术让他们露出真容。

浮士德　陛下马上就能见到这两个人。

［对靡非斯特］靡非斯特,去吧,

吹起喇叭,在庄严的音乐声中

把亚历山大和他漂亮的情人

带到这位高贵的皇帝面前。

靡非斯特　［对浮士德］遵命,浮士德。

［靡非斯特下］

班佛里奥　［在窗口］博士大人,如果你的魔鬼不快点赶

来,我可又要呼呼入睡了。真是活见鬼了,一想到我

could eat myself for anger to think I have been such an ass all this while, to stand gaping after the devil's governor and can see nothing.

FAUSTUS   [*aside*] I'll make you feel something anon, if my art fail me not.—

[*To Emperor*] My lord, I must forewarm your majesty

That when my spirits present the royal shapes

Of Alexander and his paramour,

Your grace demand no questions of the king,

But in dumb silence let them come and go.

EMPEROR   Be it as Faustus please. We are content.

BENVOLIO   [*at the window*] Ay, ay, and I am content too. An thou bring Alexander and his paramour before the emperor, I'll be Actaeon and turn myself to a stag.

FAUSTUS   [*aside*] And I'll play Diana and send you the horns presently.

   [Enter Mephistopheles. A] sennet. Enter at one [door] the Emper Alexander, at the other Darius. They meet; Darius is thrown down. Alexander kills him, takes off his crown, and, offering to go out, his Paramour meets him. He embraceth her and sets Darius' crown upon her head; and, coming back, both salute the [German] Emperor, who, leaving his state, offers to embrace them, which Faustus seeing suddenly stays him. Then trumpets cease and music sounds

My gracious lord, you do forget yourself.

These are but shadows, not substantial.

这个驴子般愚蠢的傻瓜居然一直站在这里，眼巴巴
期待着那位魔鬼的管家，结果鬼影子也不曾看见，我
真该一怒之下把自己生吞活剥了。

浮士德　[旁白]只要我的法术不失灵，

我一定要让你们大吃一惊。

[对皇帝]陛下,有句话我说在先:

当我的精灵把高贵的亚历山大

以及他的情人带到您面前,

陛下不可向这位古代帝王发问,

只能让他们在沉默中来来去去。

皇帝　一切遂浮士德所愿就是。我们很满意了。

班佛里奥　[在窗口]是啊,是啊,我也很满意呢。如果你
能把亚历山大和他的情人带到皇帝面前, 我还要做
亚克托安[30],把自己变成一头鹿呢。

浮士德　[旁白]那我就做狄安娜,马上送你一对角。

[靡非斯特重上。]喇叭响起。亚历山大大帝[自
一门]上;大流士[31]自另一门上。两人厮杀,大流
士倒地。亚历山大将他杀死, 取下他头上的王
冠,准备离开。亚历山大的情人与他会面。他拥
抱她,并将大流士的王冠戴到她头上。回转身
时,两人向[德国]皇帝致意。皇帝离座,打算拥
抱他们, 浮士德见此赶紧上前阻止。喇叭声停
止,音乐响起

陛下,你忘记自己的身份了。

他们只是影子,不是血肉之躯。

139

EMPEROR O, pardon me. My thoughts are so ravished

With sight of this renowned emperor

That in mine arms I would have compassed him.

But Faustus, since I may not speak to them

To satisfy my longing thoughts at full,

Let me this tell thee: I have heard it said

That this fair lady, whilst she lived on earth,

Had on her neck a little wart or mole.

How may I prove that saying to be true?

FAUSTUS Your majesty may boldly go and see.

EMPEROR [*making an inspection*] Faustus, I see it plain,

And in this sight thou better pleasest me

Than if I gained another monarchy.

FAUSTUS [*to the spirits*] Away, begone!

    Exit Show

See, see, my gracious lord, what strange beast is yon, that thrusts

his head out at window.

    [*Benvolio is seen to have sprouted horns*]

EMPEROR O wondrous sight! See, Duke of Saxony,

Two spreading horns most strangely fastened

Upon the head of young Benvolio.

SAXONY What, is he asleep, or dead?

FAUSTUS He sleeps, my lord, but dreams not of his horns.

EMPEROR This sport is excellent. We'll call and wake him. —

What ho, Benvolio!

140

皇帝　对不起。这著名的皇帝一出现，

　　　我的思想完全被这一景象陶醉，

　　　便情不自禁想把他揽在怀里。

　　　浮士德,既然我不能跟他说话，

　　　不能完全满足内心的仰慕之情，

　　　请你告诉我一件事:我听人说，

　　　这位漂亮的夫人活在世上时，

　　　她脖子上长有肉赘,或者说痣。

　　　这个说法怎样才能证明呢?

浮士德　陛下可以亲自上前验证。

皇帝　[查验后]浮士德,我看清楚了。

　　　我已一饱眼福,这样的喜悦

　　　不亚于让我再得一顶王冠。

浮士德　[对精灵]去,下去!

　　　　　精灵隐去

　　　陛下请看,看看上面窗口，

　　　那探头探脑的又是什么怪物?

　　　　[头上长着一对角的班佛里奥出现在窗口]

皇帝　真不可思议! 看,萨克森公爵，

　　　怪事,怪事,一对长长的大角

　　　长在年轻的班佛里奥头上呢。

萨克森　怎么,他是睡着了,还是死了?

浮士德　他睡着了,大人,只是没有梦见他的角。

皇帝　这个玩笑开得妙极了,我们叫醒他——

　　　喂,班佛里奥!

BENVOLIO   A plague upon you! Let me sleep a while.

EMPEROR   I blame thee not to sleep much, having such a head of thine own.

SAXONY   Look up, Benvolio. 'Tis the emperor calls.

BENVOLIO   The emperor? Where? O, zounds, my head!

EMPEROR   Nay, an thy horns hold. 'tis no matter for thy head, for that's armed sufficiently.

FAUSTUS   Why, how now, sir knight? What, hanged by the horns? This is most horrible. Fie, fie, pull in your head, for shame. Let not all the world wonder at you.

BENVOLIO   Zounds, doctor, is this your villainy?

FAUSTUS   O, say not so, sir. The doctor has no skills,

Nor art, no cunning to present these lords

Or bring before this royal emperor

The mighty monarch, warlike Alexander.

If Faustus do it, you are straight resolved

In bold Actaeon's shape to turn a stag.—

And therefore, my lord, so please your majesty,

I'll raise a kennel of hounds shall hurt him so

As all his footmanship shall scarce prevail

To keep is carcass from their bloody fangs.

Ho, Belimoth, Argiron, Ashtaroth!

BENVOLIO   Hold, hold! Zounds, he'll raise a kennel of devils, I think, anon. Good my lord, entreat for me. 'Sblood, I am never able to endure these torments.

142

班佛里奥 遭瘟的! 让我再睡一会。

皇帝 长了这样的一个脑袋,我们就怪不得你这么嗜睡了。

萨克森 班佛里奥,抬头看看,皇帝在跟你说话呢。

班佛里奥 皇帝？在哪里？哟,真该死,我的头!

皇帝 是的,你头上长角了,没什么要紧的,至少是一种有效的武装。

浮士德 怎么样,骑士先生？怎么,想用这对角来上吊吗？那可太可怕了。呸,呸,顾顾自己的颜面,快把脑袋缩回去吧。别让整个世界都对你大呼小叫了。

班佛里奥 该死的博士,是你在恶作剧吗？

浮士德 哟,别这么说,先生。

　　本博士才疏学浅,无才无能,

　　万难把勇武的亚历山大大帝

　　带到高贵的皇帝面前。如果

　　他有此能耐,那你得坚定意志,

　　不怕变形为亚克托安那样的雄鹿。

　　皇帝陛下,如果您有这兴致,

　　我不妨召唤一群猎狗过来追赶他,

　　让他的猎手伙伴措手不及,

　　难从嗜血的狗嘴夺下他的尸体。

　　[念咒]嗬,贝利摩斯,阿格隆,艾希塔勒斯!

班佛里奥 住口,住口! 真该死,他会把一群魔鬼招来的。好陛下,为我求求情吧。我的天,我再也受不了这样的折磨了[32]。

EMPEROR   Then, good Master Doctor,

Let me entreat you to remove his horns.

He has done penance now sufficiently.

FAUSTUS   My gracious lord, nor so much for injury done to me as to delight your majesty with some mirth hath Faustus justly requited this injurious knight; which being all I desire, I am content to remove his horns.—Mephistopheles, transform him. [*Mephistopheles removes the horns*] And hereafter, sir, look you speak well of scholars.

BENVOLIO   Speak well of ye? 'Sblood, an scholar be such cuckoldmakers to clap horns of honest men's heads o' this order, I'll ne'er trust smooth faces and small ruffs more. But, an I be not revenged for this, would I might be turned to a gaping oyster and drink nothing bu salt water.

[*Exit Benvolio from the window*]

EMPEROR   Come, Faustus. While the emperor lives,

In recompense of this thy high desert

Thou shalt command the state of Germany

Ad live beloved of mighty Carolus.

Exeunt

皇帝　好博士,

　　请你去掉他的角吧,

　　他已经得到应有的惩罚了。

浮士德　仁慈的陛下,浮士德回敬这位爱诽谤的骑士,并
不完全为了给他点颜色瞧瞧,更多的是为了让陛下
开心。如今所愿已足,我很乐意为他除去头上的角。
——靡非斯特,让他恢复原形。[靡非斯特施法消除
班佛里奥头上的角]从今往后,先生,请你对我们读
书人说话客气点。

班佛里奥　对你们说话客气点?我的天,如果读书人都是
绿头巾的制造者,动不动就在老实人的头上按一对
角,那我再也不敢相信戴皱领子、皮肤光滑的人了。
此仇不报,我就是一个张开大口的牡蛎,靠咸水维持
生命。

　　　　[班佛里奥从窗口下]

皇帝　来吧,浮士德。只要我活着,

　　你创造的奇迹就铭记在我心中,

　　你可以号令整个德意志帝国,

　　强大的理查永远把你崇敬。

　　　　同下

SCENE 2

Enter Benvolio, Martino, Frederick, and Soldiers

MARTINO Nay, sweet Benvolio, let us sway thy thoughts

From this attempt against the conjurer.

BENVOLIO Away! You love me not, to urge me thus.

Shall I let slip so great an injury

When every servile groom jests at my wrongs

And in their rustic gambols proudly say,

'Benvolio's head was graced with horns today'?

O, may these eyelids never close again

Till with my sword I have that conjurer slain!

If you will aid me in this enterprise,

Then draw your weapons and be resolute.

If not, depart. Here will Benvolio die

But Faustus' death shall quit my infamy.

FREDERICK Nay, we will stay with thee, betide what may,

And kill that doctor if he come this way.

BENVOLIO Then, gentle Frederick, hie thee to the grove,

And place our servants and our followers

Close in an ambush there behind the trees.

第二场

班佛里奥、马丁诺、弗雷德里克、若干兵士上

马丁诺　亲爱的班佛里奥,我们还是

打消刺杀魔法师的念头吧。

班佛里奥　你走吧! 你不爱我,才会说这话。

如此奇耻大辱,我怎能容忍?

每一个仆役都在嘲笑我,

他们扯着粗俗的嗓门嚷嚷:

"班佛里奥今天戴绿头巾了!"

我要用这剑杀了那个魔法师,

不达目的,我是死不瞑目的。

如果你愿意助我一臂之力,

请你拔出宝剑,坚定信心。

不然,请走开。我即便拼了性命,

也要杀了浮士德以雪我的耻辱。

弗雷德里克　不管发生什么,我们都跟你在一起,

只要博士走过这里,他必死无疑。

班佛里奥　好弗雷德里克,快去树林里

藏起来,我们的仆人和跟班

都到树底下埋伏。我知道,

By this, I know, the conjurer is near;

I saw him kneel and kiss the emperor's hand

And take his leave, laden with rich rewards.

Then, soldiers, boldly fight. If Faustus die,

Take you the wealth; leave us the victory.

FREDERICK Come, soldiers, follow me unto the grove.

Who kills him shall have gold and endless love.

Exit Frederick with the Soldiers

BENVOLIO My head is lighter than it was by th'horns

But yet my heart's more ponderous than my head

And pants until I see the conjurer dead.

MARTINO Where shall we place ourselves, Benvolio?

BENVOLIO Here will we stay to bide the first assult.

O, were that damned hellhound but in place,

Thou soon shouldst see me quit my foul disgrace.

Enter Frederick

FREDERICK Close, close! The conjurer is at hand

And all alone comes walking in his gown.

Be ready, then, and strike the peasant down.

BENVOLIO Mine be that honour, then. Now, sword, strike home!

For horns he gave, I'll have his head anon.

Enter Faustus, with the false head

MARTINO See, see, he comes.

BENVOLIO   No word. This blow ends all.

Hell take his soul! His body thus must fall.

148

魔法师不一会就要来到这里。

刚才我看见他跪吻皇帝的手，

满载着种种奖赏向他道别。

士兵们，勇敢作战！浮士德一死，

财富就全归你们，我们只要胜利。

弗雷德里克　来吧，士兵们，跟我进树林。

谁杀了他，谁获金币和爱慕。

弗雷德里克率兵士下

班佛里奥　摘下角的脑袋固然轻松，

但此刻我的心却无比沉重，

只因魔法师尚未挨刀命终。

马丁诺　我们自己藏哪里，班佛里奥？

班佛里奥　我和你就在这里等着他，

这地狱的恶狗一旦出现，

你就看我如何报仇雪恨吧。

弗雷德里克上

弗雷德里克　别出声！魔法师过来了！

他身披长袍，只身一人。

做好准备，撂倒这个乡巴佬。

班佛里奥　荣誉是我的。就一剑封喉！

他戴我绿头巾，我要他的命。

装着假脑袋的浮士德上

马丁诺　看，看，他过来了。

班佛里奥　别说话。这一剑算总账。

下地狱去吧！看你倒不倒下来。

149

[He strikes Faustus]

FAUSTUS   *[falling]* O!

FREDERICK   Groan you, Master Doctor?

BENVOLIO   Break may his heart with groans! Dear Frederick, see,

Thus will I end his griefs immediately.

MARTINO   Strike with a willing hand.

[Benvolio strikes off Faustus' false head]

His head is off!

BENVOLIO   The devil's dead. The Furies now may laugh.

FREDERICK   Was this that stern aspect, that awful frown,

Made the grim monarch of infernal spirits

Tremble and quake at his commanding charms?

MARTINO   Was this that damned head whose heart conspired

Benvolio's shame before the emperor?

BENVOLIO   Ay, that's the head and here the body lies,

Just rewarded for his villainies.

FREDERICK   Come, let's devise how we may add more shame

To the black scandal of his hatred name.

BENVOLIO   First, on his head, in quittance of my wrongs,

I'll nail huge forked horns and let them hang

Within the window where he yoked me first,

That all the world may see my just revenge.

MARTINO   What use shall we put his beard to?

BENVOLIO   We'll sell it to a chimney-sweeper. It will wear out ten birchen

brooms, I warrant you.

[刺向浮士德]

浮士德 [倒地]哎哟!

弗雷德里克 博士,你在呻吟吗?

班佛里奥 让他呻吟到心碎吧! 亲爱的弗雷德里克,
看好了,我即刻解除他的痛苦。

马丁诺 赶紧砍。

[班佛里奥砍下浮士德的假脑袋]

头砍下了?

班佛里奥 魔鬼死了。复仇女神可以笑了。

弗雷德里克 这就是那个板着面孔、皱紧眉头,
神气活现地念咒,连总管阴间精灵的
魔王撒旦见了都索索直抖的魔法师吗?

马丁诺 就是这个该死的家伙挖空心思,
在皇帝面前制造班佛里奥的耻辱吗?

班佛里奥 不错,正是他,地上是他的尸体,
他的恶行已经得到应有的报应了。

弗雷德里克 来,我们想点办法,让"浮士德"
这个可恶的名字再添点耻辱。

班佛里奥 首先,作为回报,我要在他头上
装一对分叉的角,然后挂到我曾经
受困过的那个窗口,这样,全世界
都知道我出了一口恶气了。

马丁诺 他的胡子能派点什么用场?

班佛里奥 把它卖给扫烟囱的。我向你保证,用它扫烟
囱,一定抵得上十把桦条扫帚。

FREDERICK   What shall his eyes do?

BENVOLIO   We'll put out his eyes, and they shall serve for buttons to his
lips to keep his tongue from catching cold.

MARTINO   An excellent policy. And now, sirs, having divided him,
what shall the body do?

[Faustus rises]

BENVOLIO   Zounds, the devil's alive again!

FREDERICK   Give him his head, for God's sake!

FAUSTUS   Nay, keep it. Faustus will have heads and hands,

Ay, all your hearts, to recompense this deed.

Knew you not, traitors, I was limited

For four-and-twenty years to breathe on earth?

And had you cut my body with your swords,

Or hewed this flesh and bones as small as sand,

Yet in a minute had my spirit returned,

And I had breathed a man made free from harm.

But wherefore do I dally my revenge?

Ashtoroth, Belimoth, Mephistopheles!

Enter Mephistopheles and other Devils [Belimoth and Ashtaroth]

Go horse these traitors on your fiery backs,

And mount aloft with them as high as heaven;

Thence pitch them headlong to the lowest hell.

Yet stay. The world shall see their misery,

And hell after plague their treachery.

Go, Belimoth, and take this caitiff hence,

弗雷德里克　他的眼珠子如何处置？

班佛里奥　把他的眼珠子挖出来，用作扣子，封住他的
　　嘴，以免他的舌头受凉。

马丁诺　绝妙的主意。来吧，先生们，现在就动手。这无头
　　尸体怎么办？

　　　　　[浮士德从地上爬起]

班佛里奥　哎呀呀，魔鬼复活了！

弗雷德里克　看在上帝的分上，把头还给他！

浮士德　你们留着吧。浮士德有的是头和手，
　　对了，作为酬谢，他需要你们所有人的心。
　　恶贼，在这个世界上，我的寿限
　　还有二十四年，这你们不知道吧？
　　即便你们用刀剑把我切成两半，
　　或者干脆将我的骨肉剁成肉酱，
　　我的灵魂也能即刻从阴府返回，
　　恢复生命的形态，毫发未损。
　　咳，我干吗不赶紧报仇呢？
　　艾希塔勒斯，贝利摩斯，靡非斯特！

　　　靡非斯特偕其他魔鬼[贝利摩斯、艾希塔勒斯]上
　　用你们燃烧着的背扛起这些恶贼，
　　带着他们高高飞上天空，
　　然后倒栽葱般摔进地狱深渊。
　　等一等！我得让世人看见他们的痛苦，
　　地狱将因他们的罪恶瘟疫肆虐。
　　贝利摩斯，你带走这个卑鄙小人，

153

And hurl him in some lake of mud and dirt.

[*To Ashtaroth*]

Take thou this other; drag him through the woods

Amongst the pricking thorns and sharpest briers,

Whilst with my gentle Mephistopheles

This traitor flies unto some steepy rock

That, rolling down, may break the villain's bones

As he intend to dismember me.

Fly hence. Dispatch my charge immediately.

FREDERICK   Pity us, gentle Faustus. Save our lives!

FAUSTUS   Away!

FREDERICK   He must needs go that the devil drives.

> *Exeunt Spirits with the Knights on their backs. Enter the*
> *ambushed Soldiers*

FIRST SOLDIER   Come, sirs. Prepare yourself in readiness;

Make haste to help these noble gentlemen,

I heard them parley with the conjurer.

SECOND SOLDIER   See where he comes. Dispatch, and kill the slave.

FAUSTUS   What's here? An ambush to betray my life?

Then, Faustus, try thy skill. Base peasants, stand!

For lo, these trees remove at my command

And stand as bulwarks 'twixt yourselves and me

To shield me from your hatred treachery.

Yet to encounter this your weak attempt,

Behold an army comes incontinent.

把他丢进臭气熏天的泥塘。

    [对艾希塔勒斯]

你负责这一位:把他拖进树林,

让他的身体在荆棘丛中穿行。

亲爱的靡菲斯特,你对付这位奸贼,

带他飞到某处悬崖峭壁上,让他

从山顶滚下,滚断他的骨头,

就像他图谋肢解我那样。

飞去吧。立即执行我的命令!

弗雷德里克 可怜可怜我们吧,好浮士德,饶命吧。

浮士德 去!

弗雷德里克 唉,魔鬼当前,只好听天由命了。

    魔鬼将三骑士扛肩上下;

    设伏的兵士上

兵士甲 同伴们,来,大家做好战斗准备,

赶紧帮帮那几位高贵的骑士。

我听见他们在跟魔法师说话。

兵士乙 他过来了。快,杀了这个奴才。

浮士德 怎么,你们埋伏在此想害我啊?

浮士德,该出手了。乡巴佬,站住!

你们看好,这些树听我的号令,

乖乖来到这里,形成一堵屏障,

保护我不被你们的奸计所伤。

为对付你们这小小的伎俩,

还有一支大军马上赶来现场。

Faustus strikes the door, and enter a Devil playing on a drum, after him another bearing an ensign, and divers with weapons; Mephistopheles with fireworks. They set upon the Soldiers and drive them out. [Exit Faustus]

浮士德敲门,众魔上。一魔击鼓,一魔举旗,还有一魔手持武器。靡非斯特手握烟花。他们一齐向兵士进攻,兵士逃走,众魔追下。[浮士德跟着下]

SCENE 3

Enter at several doors Benvolio, Frederick, and Martino,
their heads and faces bloody and besmeared with mud and
dirt, all having horns on their heads

MARTINO   What ho, Benvolio!

BENVOLIO   Here. What, Frederick, ho!

FREDERICK   O, help me, gentle friend. Where is Martino?

MARTINNO   Dear Frederick, here,

Half smothered in a lake of mud and dirt

Through which the Furies dragged me by the heels.

FREDERICK   Martino, see! Benvolio's horns again.

MARTINNO   O misery! How now, Benvolio?

BENVOLIO   Defend me, heaven. Shall I be haunted still?

MARTINNO   Nay, fear not, man. We have no power to kill.

BENVOLIO   My friend transformed thus! O hellish spite!

Your heads are all set with horns.

FREDERICK   You hit it right.

It is your own you mean. Feel on your head.

BENVOLIO   [*feeling his head*] Zounds, horns again.

MARTINNO   Nay, chafe not, man, we all are sped.

第三场

　　　　　　班佛里奥、弗雷德里克、马丁诺各自上,他们都
　　　　　　血流满面,浑身沾满泥浆和污垢。每个人头上都
　　　　　　长出了角

马丁诺　　哎哟哟,班佛里奥!

班佛里奥　　我在这里。弗雷德里克呢,哎哟哟!

弗雷德里克　　救救我吧,好朋友,马丁诺呢?

马丁诺　　亲爱的弗雷德里克,我在这里。

　　　　复仇神抓住我的脚后跟,拖过

　　　　满是淤泥的臭水湖,我都快憋死了。

弗雷德里克　　马丁诺,你看! 班佛里奥又长角了。

马丁诺　　真惨啊! 怎么了,班佛里奥?

班佛里奥　　老天爷,救救我。魔鬼还在作祟吗?

马丁诺　　别怕,老弟。我们不会死的。

班佛里奥　　我的朋友怎么变成这样!

　　　　真可恶啊! 你们头上都长角了。

弗雷德里克　　你说得不错,你是在说自己。

　　　　摸摸你自己的头吧。

班佛里奥　　[摸了摸头]该死,又长角了!

马丁诺　　别发火,老兄,神会保佑我们的。

BENVOLIO   What devil attends this damned magician,

That, spite of spite, our wrongs are doubled?

FREDERICK   What may we do, that we may hide our shames?

BENVOLIO   If we should follow him to work revenge,

He'd join long asses' ear to these huge horns

And make us laughing-stocks to all the world.

MARTINNO   What shall we then do, dear Benvolio?

BENVOLIO   I have a castle joining near these woods,

And thither we'll repair and live obscure

Till time shall alter this our brutish shapes.

Sith black disgrace hath thus eclipsed our fame,

We'll rather die with grief than live with shame.

Exeunt

班佛里奥　侍候该死的魔法师的魔鬼是谁？

　　　是谁害得我们枉费心机,一错再错？

弗雷德里克　我们怎么办好呢？这耻辱如何掩饰呢？

班佛里奥　如果我们跟踪他,图谋报复,

　　　他定会在我们角上再添一对驴耳,

　　　让我们成为普天下人的笑柄。

马丁诺　我们到底怎么办好,亲爱的班佛里奥？

班佛里奥　我知道有座城堡就在树林边,

　　　我们上那里住下,从此隐姓埋名,

　　　直到时间将我们丑恶的形貌改变。

　　　奇耻大辱已经使我们名誉扫地,

　　　与其含辱偷生,不如一死了之。

　　　　同下

SCENE 4

Enter Faustus, and the Horse-courser, and Mephistopheles

HORSE-COURSER [*offering money*]

I beseech your worship, accept of these forty dollars.

FAUSTUS Friend, thou canst not buy so good a horse for so small a price. I have no great need to sell him, but if thou likest him for ten dollars more, take him, because I see thou hast a good mind to him.

HORSE-COURSER I beseech you, sir, accept of this. I am a very poor man and have lost very much of late by horseflesh, and this bargain will set me up again.

FAUSTUS Well, I will not stand with thee. Give me the money. [*He takes the money*] Now, sirrah, I must tell you that you may ride him o'er hedge and ditch, and spare him not. But do you hear? In any case ride him not into the water.

HORSE-COURSER How, sir, not into the water? Why, will he not drink of all waters?

FAUSTUS Yes, he will drink of all waters. But ride him not into the water. O'er hedge and ditch, or where thou wilt, but not into the water. Go bid the ostler deliver him unto you, and remember what I say.

第四场

浮士德、马贩、靡非斯特上

马贩 ［递钱］

请阁下收下这四十元吧。

浮士德 朋友,这么低的价格,你是买不到这么好的一匹马的。我也不急于卖这匹马;如果你真的喜欢它,那就再加十元让你牵走,因为我看得出,你是真正看上了这匹马。

马贩 先生,我求你就按这个数成交吧。我是个穷人,最近卖马肉又亏了许多。这笔交易就当您扶助我吧。

浮士德 好吧,我也不跟你斤斤计较了,把钱给我。［接过钱］伙计,我得告诉你:这马你尽可以骑着跨篱笆,过壕沟,但你听好了,无论如何不可以骑它下水。

马贩 怎么,先生,你说这匹马不可以下水?难道它不喝水吗?

浮士德 水是要喝的。但不可以骑它到水里去。跨篱笆,过壕沟,都随你的便,就是不可以下水。去吧,让饲马的把马交给你。记住我说过的话。

HORSE-COURSER   I warrant you, sir.—O, joyful day! Now am I a made man for ever.

Exit [Horse-courser]

FAUSTUS   What are thou, Faustus, but a man condemned to die?

Thy fatal time draws to a final end.

Despair doth drive distrust into my thoughts.

Confound these passions with a quiet sleep.

Tush! Christ did call the thief upon the cross;

Then rest thee, Faustus quiet in conceit.

He sits to sleep. Enter the Horse-courser, wet

HORSE-COURSER   O, what a cozening doctor was this! I, riding my horse into the water, thinking some hidden misery had been in the horse, I had nothing under me but a little straw and had much ado to escape drowning. Well, I'll go rouse him and make him give me my forty dollars again.—Ho, sirrah doctor, you cozening scab! Master Doctor, awake, and rise, and give me my money again, for your horse is turned to a bottle of hay. Master Doctore! [*He pulls off his leg*] Alas, I am undone! What shall I do? I have pulled off his leg.

FAUSTUS   O, help, help! The villain hath murdered me.

HORSE-COURSER   Murder or not murder, now he has but one leg I'll outrun him and cast this leg into some ditch or other.

[Exit Horse-courser with the leg]

FAUSTUS   Stop him, stop him, stop him!—Ha, ha, ha! Faustus hath his leg again, and the Horse-courser a bundle of hay for his forty

马贩 没问题,先生。——真开心的一天! 但愿我永远走好运。

    [马贩子]下

浮士德 浮士德哟,你不是注定要死的人吗?

你的大限步步逼近,几临终点。

绝望不断将疑虑灌注我的心胸。

让安静的睡眠平息纷扰的思绪吧。

唪! 基督在十字架上还与强盗打招呼呢;

浮士德,好好歇息吧,别胡思乱想了。

    浮士德在椅子上睡了过去。马贩上,浑身湿透

马贩 好一个骗子博士! 我骑着马进入水中,原以为这马有什么神秘的地方, 谁想胯下的马竟成了一把麦秆, 我费了很大的劲才避免淹死。我要过去叫醒他,让他还我那四十元。——喂,博士先生,你这骗人的恶棍! 博士大师,快醒醒,快起来,把钱还给我, 你的马已经变成一把麦秆了。博士大师! [马贩开始拽浮士德的腿,结果腿被拽断]哎呀呀,我这下完了! 看我做了什么了? 我把他的腿拉断了。

浮士德 哎哟,救命啊,救命! 这个恶棍把我谋杀了。

马贩 谋不谋杀不管它, 反正他只有一条腿,追不上我的,赶紧把他的断腿丢到阴沟里去。

    [马贩抱断腿逃下]

浮士德 抓住他,抓住他,抓住他! ——哈,哈,哈! 浮士德又长出一条腿来了,这马贩子花了四十元,换得一

dollars.

Enter Wagner

How now, Wagner, what news with thee?

WAGNER   If it please you, the duke of Vanholt doth earnestly entreat your company and hath sent some of his men to attend you with provision fit for your journey.

FAUSTUS   The duke of Vanholt's an honourable gentleman, and one to whom I must be no niggard of my cunning. Come away.

Exeunt

把麦秆。

　　　　瓦格纳上

怎么啦,瓦格纳,你有什么消息?

瓦格纳　先生,打扰一下,凡豪特公爵向您发出诚挚的邀
　　请。他还派了人来,带足了路上所需的一切,准备侍
　　候您。

浮士德　凡豪特公爵德高望重,这样的贵人邀请我,我是
　　不可怠慢的。走吧。

　　　　同下

SCENE 5

Enter Clown [Robin], Dick, Horse-courser and a Carter

CARTER Come, my masters, I'll bring you to the best beer in Europe.—
What ho, Hostess!—Where be these whores?

Enter Hostess

HOSTESS How now, what lack you? What, my old guests, welcome!

ROBIN [*aside to Dick*] Sirrah Dick, dost thou know why I stand so
mute?

DICK [*aside to Robin*] No, Robin, why is't?

ROBIN [*aside to Dick*] I am eighteen pence on the score. But say
nothing. See if she have forgotten me.

HOSTESS [*seeing Robin*] Who's this that stands so solemnly by himself?
[*To Robin*] What, my old guest?

ROBIN O, Hostess, how do you? I hope my score stands still.

HOSTESS Ay, there's no doubt of that, for methinks you make no haste
to wipe it out.

DICK Why, Hostess, I say, fetch us some beer.

HOSTESS You shall, presently.—Look up into th' hall there, ho!

Exit [Hostess]

DICK Come, sirs, what shall we do now till mine Hostess comes?

第五场

小丑[罗宾]、迪克、马贩、马车夫上

马车夫　各位，我要带你们去尝尝欧洲最好的啤酒。
　　——喂,老板娘! 老板娘! ——这班婊子去哪儿了?

女店主上

女店主　你们要点什么？哟,都是老顾客,欢迎欢迎!

罗宾　[对迪克]迪克伙计,你知道我为什么一言不发地
　　站着吗?

迪克　[对罗宾]不知道。怎么回事,罗宾?

罗宾　[对迪克]我在她的账上还欠着十八个便士呢。你
　　千万别说出来。先看看她是否忘了这笔账。

女店主　[看见罗宾]这位板着脸一直站着的先生是谁
　　啊？哟,不是我的老顾客吗?

罗宾　喔喔,老板娘,你好。我想让那笔赊账再挂挂。

女店主　好的,这没问题,照我看来,你也用不着急于抹
　　掉它呀。

迪克　老板娘,给我们来点啤酒。

女店主　好,稍等。——喂,看看厅那边的顾客要点什么!

[女店主]下

迪克　来,伙计,啤酒还没上来,我们现在能做点什么呢?

CARTER   Marry, sir, I'll tell you the bravest tale how a conjurer served me. You know Doctor Faustus?

HORSE-COURSER   Ay, a plague take him! Here's some on's have cause to know him. Did he conjure thee, too?

CARTER   I'll tell you how he served me. As I was going to Wittenberg t'other day with a load of hay, he met me and asked me what he should give me for as much hay as he could eat. Now, sir, I thinking that a little would serve his turn, bade him take as much as he would for three farthings. So he presently gave me my money and fell to eating; and, as I am a cursen man, he never left eating till he had eat up all my load of hay.

ALL   O monstrous! Eat a whole load of hay!

ROBIN   Yes, yes, that may be, for I have heard of one that has eat a load of logs.

HORSE-COURSER   Now, sirs, you shall hear how villainously he served me. I went to him yesterday to buy a horse of him, and he would by no means sell him under forty dollars. So, sir, because I knew him to be such a horse as would run over hedge and ditch and never tire, I gave him his money. So when I had my horse, Doctor Faustus bade me ride him night and day and spare him no time. 'But', quoth he, 'in any case ride him not into the water.' Now, sir, I, thinking the horse had had some quality that he would not have me know of, what did I but rid him into a great river? And when I came just in the midst, my horse vanished away, and I sat straddling upon a bottle of hay.

马车夫　先生,让我来告诉你们一件最最奇怪的事,我曾经上过一位魔法师的当。你们认识浮士德这个人吗?

马贩　让他遭瘟去吧!这里就有人认识他。难道他对你也施过魔法?

马车夫　我告诉你们他怎样骗我。那天我装了一车干草去维腾堡,他碰到我就问,如果我的一车子干草让他吃,他得付多少钱。我想,这回可轮到他上我的当了,就对他说,只要他付三个法新[33],我的干草他可以尽量吃。他听了我的话,马上交给我三个铜币,开始吃干草。我是个基督徒,说话算话,只能眼巴巴看着他把我的一车干草全吃光了。

众人　哇,真是神奇!吃一车干草!

罗宾　不错,不错,这是有可能的,我还听说有人吃过一车木头呢。

马贩　伙计,你们再听我说说这个恶棍是如何骗人的吧。昨天我去见他,向他买马,若马的价格少于四十元,他无论如何不愿成交。伙计,我知道那是一匹好马,跳个篱笆跨个壕沟什么的,从来不累,因此我便给了他四十元钱。我得到这匹马后,浮士德博士关照我说:这马我日日夜夜骑都行。"但是,"他说,"无论如何不可以骑到水里。"伙计,我当时就想:这马一定有什么秘密是他不愿向我透露的,我偏要骑到大河里去试试。当我骑着马来到河中央,这马消失不见了,胯下只剩下一捆干草!

ALL   O brave doctor!

HORSE-COURSER   But you shall hear how bravely I served him for it. I went me home to his house, and there I found him asleep. I kept a halloing and whooping in his ears, but all could not wake him. I, seeing that, took him by the leg and never rested pulling till I had pulled me his leg quite off, and now 'tis at home in mine hostry.

ROBIN   And has the doctor but one leg, then? That's excellent, for one of his devils turned me into the likeness of an ape's face.

CARTER   Some more drink, Hostess!

ROBIN   Hark you, we'll into another room and drink a while, and then we'll go seek out the doctor.

    Exeunt

众人 神奇的博士!

马贩 你们再听我说说而后发生的更神奇的事。我到他的住处找他,发现他在呼呼大睡。我便在他耳边喂喂喂大声呼喊,但始终叫不醒他。见他那个样子,我便握住他的一条腿不停地拽, 结果就把他的腿给拽下来了。这条腿现在还在我家的马房里呢。

罗宾 这么说博士只有一条腿了?这太好了!他的一个魔鬼还把我变成过一只猴子呢。

马车夫 再给我们来几杯,老板娘!

罗宾 来吧!我们到另一间房里喝吧,喝完后我们就去找博士。

　　　　同下

SCENE 6

*Enter the Duke of Vanholt, his [pregnant] Duchess, Faustus,
and Mephistopheles [and Servants]*

DUKE   Thanks, Master Doctor, for these pleasant sights. Not know I
how sufficiently to recompense your great deserts in erecting that
enchanted castle in the air, the sight whereof so delighted me as
nothing in the world could please me more.

FAUSTUS   I do think myself, my good lord, highly recompensed in that
it pleaseth your grace to think but well of that which Faustus hath
performed.—But, gracious lady, it may be that you have taken no
pleasure in those sights. Therefore, I pray you tell me what is the
thing you most desire to have; be it in the world, it shall be yours. I
have heard that great-bellied women do long for things are rare and
dainty.

DUCHESS   True, Master Doctor, and, since I find you so kind, I will
make known unto you what my heart desires to have. And were it
now summer, as it is January, a dead time of the winter, I would
request no better meat than a dish of ripe grapes.

FAUSTUS   This is but a small matter. [*Aside to Mephistopheles*] Go,
Mephistopheles, away!

第六场

凡豪特公爵、[怀孕的]公爵夫人、浮士德、靡非斯特及若干仆役上

公爵 博学的大师,谢谢您为我们展示这一切。您凭魔法建造出空中城堡,普天下再没有比这更赏心悦目的美妙场景了,我真不知道如何报答您的旷世奇功。

浮士德 阁下,浮士德的雕虫小技能取悦于您,得到您的嘉许,对我来说便是最好的回报了。——仁慈的夫人,这些场景好像并未博得您的欢心,请您告诉我,什么东西是您最想得到的。只要是这个世界所具有的,我都能为您觅到。我曾听说,有孕在身的女子通常都希望得到稀有珍宝。

公爵夫人 这倒也是,博学的大师。既然您对我如此友好,我也不妨让您知道内心的渴求了。眼下是寒冬腊月,如果是夏天就好了:我不稀罕山珍海味,只要一盘子熟透的葡萄。

浮士德 这不过是举手之劳。[对靡非斯特]走吧,靡非斯特,快去!

Exit Mephistopheles

Madam, I will do more than this for your content.

Enter Mephistopheles again with the grapes

Here. Now taste ye these. They should be good, for they come from a far country, I can tell you.

[*The Duchess tastes the grapes*]

DUKE   This makes me wonder more than all the rest, that at this time of the year, when every tree is barren of his fruits, from whence you had these ripe grapes.

FAUSTUS   Please it your grace, the year is divided into two circles over the whole world, so that, when it is winter with us, in the contrary circle it is likewise summer with them, as in India, Saba and such countries that lie far east, where they have fruit twice a year. From whence, by means of a swift spirit that I have, I had these grapes brought, as you see.

DUCHESS   And, trust me, they are the sweetest grapes that e'er I tasted.

The Clown[s] bounce at the gate, within

DUKE   What rude disturbers have we at the gate?

Go pacify their fury. Set it ope,

And then demand of them what they would have.

They knock again and call out to talk with Faustus

SERVANT   [*calling offstage*]

Why, how now, masters, what a coil is there!

What is the reason you disturb the duke?

DICK   [*offstage*] We have no reason for it. Therefore, a fig for him!

176

靡非斯特下

夫人,为了让您满意,您可以吩咐我做点其他的事。

　　靡非斯特端上一盘鲜葡萄

葡萄来了,夫人请尝。这是很好的葡萄,产自很遥远的一个国家。

　　[公爵夫人品尝葡萄]

公爵　这可真让我感到万分惊奇：每年这个时候,万木萧疏,果实无存,这熟透的葡萄你是从哪里摘取的呢?

浮士德　公爵阁下,我们这个地球分成两个半球,当我们这里处于冬季时,另一半球就处在夏季,印度、示巴,以及在遥远东方的那些国家都是,因此,每年的水果就有两熟了。你现在见到的这些葡萄,就是我打发我的一个能日行千里的精灵,从地球那边取来的。

公爵夫人　相信我,这是我吃过最甜的葡萄。

　　后台传来猛烈的敲门声

公爵　是谁那般无礼,把门敲得震天价响?

去,让他们安静点。把门打开,

问问他们,他们上这里来有什么事?

　　敲门声再起,要求浮士德出来说话

仆役　[对后台]

喂,你们在那里吵什么!

你们干吗来打扰公爵大人?

迪克　[后台]我们不干吗。有点小事找他!

SERVANT   Why, saucy varlets, dare you be so bold?

HORSE-COURSER   [*offstage*] I hope, sir, we have wit enough to be more bold than welcome.

SERVANT   It appears so. Pray be bold elsewhere, and trouble not the duke.

DUKE   [*to the Servant*] What would they have?

SERVANT   They all cry out to speak with Doctor Faustus.

CARTER   [*offstage*] Ay, and we will speak with him.

DUKE   Will you, sir? —Commit the rascals.

DICK   [*offstage*] Commit with us? He were so good commit with his father as commit with us.

FAUSTUS   I do beseech your grace, let them come in.

They are good subject for a merriment.

DUKE   Do as thou wilt, Faustus. I give thee leave.

FAUSTUS   I thank your grace.

[*The Servant opens the gate.*] *Enter the Clown   [Robin], Dick, Carter, and Horse-courser*

Why, how now, my good friends?

'Faith, you are too outrageous. But come near;

I have procured your pardons. Welcome all!

ROBIN   Nay, sir, we will be welcome for our money, and we will pay for what we take.—What ho! Give's half a dozen of beer here, and be hanged.

FAUSTUS   Nay, hark you, can you tell me where you are?

CARTER   Ay, marry, can I. We are under heaven.

仆役 无礼的混蛋,敢在这里撒野吗?

马贩 [后台]我说,先生,我们有足够的理由撒点野,用不着感激什么人。

仆役 好像是这么回事。恳请你们到别处撒野去,别打扰公爵。

公爵 [对仆役]他们有何贵干?

仆役 他们嚷嚷着要跟浮士德说话。

马车夫 [后台]对了,我们要跟他说话。

公爵 是吗?——该进监狱的恶徒!

迪克 [后台]我们进监狱?该进监狱的是浮士德和他的父亲,不是我们。

浮士德 公爵阁下,您就让他们进来吧。

这班人可以为您添点乐子的。

公爵 那就按你的意思办吧,浮士德。一切由你决定。

浮士德 多谢阁下。

[仆役开门]小丑罗宾、迪克、马车夫、马贩上。

你们好啊,我的好朋友们!

你们确实太鲁莽了。走近一点。

我已请求公爵原谅你们。欢迎诸位!

罗宾 好,先生,我们只要有钱,就受欢迎。上什么,我们就付什么。——好哇! 给我们再来半打啤酒,然后大家上吊去。[34]

浮士德 听好了:你们知道这里是什么地方吗?

马车夫 老天爷,我来回答:我们就在天空底下。

179

SERVANT Ay, but, sir saucebox, know you in what place?

HORSE-COURSER Ay, ay, the house is good enough to drink in. Zounds, fill us some beer, or we'll break all the barrels in the house and dash out all your brains with your bottles.

FAUSTUS Be not so furious. Come, you shall have beer.—

My lord, beseech you give me leave a while.

I'll gage my credit 'twill content your grace.

DUKE With all my heart, kind doctor. Please thyself.

Our servants and our court's at thy command.

FAUSTUS I humbly thank your grace.—Then fetch some beer.

HORSE-COURSER Ay, marry, there spake a doctor indeed, and, 'faith, I'll drink a health to thy wooden leg for that word.

FAUSTUS My wooden leg? What dost thou mean by that?

CARTER Ha, ha, ha! Dost hear hi, Dick? He has forgot his leg.

HORSE-COURSER Ay, ay. He does not stand much upon that.

FAUSTUS No, 'faith, not much upon a wooden leg.

CARTER Good Lord, that flesh and blood should be so frail with your worship! Do not you remember a horse-courser you sold a horse to?

FAUSTUS Yes, I remember I sold one a horse.

CARTER And do you remember you bid he should not ride into the water?

FAUSTUS Yes, I do very well remember that.

CARTER And do you remember nothing of your leg?

FAUSTUS No, in good sooth.

CARTER Then, I pray, remember your curtsy.

180

仆役　无礼的家伙,你不知道这是什么地方吗?

马贩　谁不知道,这是个喝酒的好地方。少说废话,给我们倒酒,否则就把这里的瓶瓶罐罐全砸烂,然后再用酒瓶子砸你们的脑门。

浮士德　别气势汹汹的。来,我给你们上酒。

公爵阁下,请允许我跟他们说说话,

我以名誉担保,阁下一定玩得开心。

公爵　我的好博士,去吧,你请便就是。

我的用人和整个爵府都听命于你。

浮士德　敬谢公爵阁下。——快拿啤酒来!

马贩　嗨,说话的正是博士本人。真的,为你这句话,我要干一杯,祝你的木头腿健康长寿!

浮士德　我的木头腿?这话从何说起?

马车夫　哈,哈,哈!你听见了吗,迪克?他忘记自己的腿了。

马贩　当然,当然,他用不着木头腿。

浮士德　是的,我确实不需要木头腿。

马车夫　我的天,阁下真够健忘!你不记得一个马贩子向你买过一匹马了?

浮士德　记得,我是卖过一匹马。

马车夫　你嘱咐那个买马的,让他不要把马骑进水里,这你还记得不?

浮士德　记得很清楚。

马车夫　那你就一点也不记得自己的腿了?

浮士德　真的,一点也不记得。

马车夫　求你,行个屈膝礼。[35]

181

FAUSTUS [*making a curtsy*] I thank you, sir.

CARTER 'Tis not so much worth. I pray you tell me one thing.

FAUSTUS What's that?

CARTER Be both your legs bedfellows every night together?

FAUSTUS Wouldest thou make a Colossus of me, that thou askest me such questions?

CARTER No, truly, sir, I would make nothing of you. But I would fain know that.

    Enter Hostess with drink

FAUSTUS Then, I assure thee, certainly they are.

CARTER I thank you. I am fully satisfied.

FAUSTUS But wherefore dost thou ask?

CARTER For nothing, sir. But methinks you should have a wooden bedfellow of one of 'em.

HORSE-COURSER Why, do you hear, sir? Did not I pull off one of your legs when you were asleep?

FAUSTUS But I have it again now I am awake. Look you here, sir.

    [*He shows them his legs*]

ALL O, horrible! Had the doctor three legs?

CARTER Do you remember, sir, how you cozened me and eat up my load of—

    [*Faustus charms him dumb*]

DICK Do you remember how you made me wear an ape's—

    [*Faustus charms him dumb*]

HORSE-COURSER You whoreson conjuring scab, do you remember how

182

浮士德 [行屈膝礼]多谢了,先生。

马车夫 这个屈膝礼行得不地道。请你告诉我一件事。

浮士德 你说。

马车夫 你睡觉时,床上还有两条腿吗?

浮士德 你向我提这样的问题, 是不是把我当童话中的巨人了?

马车夫 没有,先生,我没有把你当巨人。我只是想把事情弄弄清楚。

       女店主带酒上

浮士德 你都看见了,这下清楚了吧。

马车夫 谢谢你。我满意了。

浮士德 你为什么要问这个?

马车夫 不为什么,先生。我原本以为你的一条腿一定是木头装的。

马贩 你听见了吗,先生?当你睡觉时,你的一条腿不是被我拉断了吗?

浮士德 我一苏醒,我的腿就长回去了。你们看看吧。

       [浮士德露腿示于众人]

众人 了不得啊! 博士该不会有三条腿吧?

马车夫 先生,你记得我吗,我就是那个上过你的当,被你吃了一马车——

       [浮士德念咒,使马车夫噤声]

迪克 你记得我吗,你把我变成了一只猴——

       [浮士德念起咒语,使迪克噤声]

马贩 你这招魂唤鬼的无赖私生子,你记得我吗,你骗我

you conzened me with a ho—

    [Faustus charms him dumb]

ROBIN   Ha' you forgotten me?   You think to carry it away with your 'hey-pass' and 'repass'. Do you remember the dog's fa—

    [Faustus charms him dumb] Exeunt Clowns

HOSTESS   Who pays for the ale?   Hear you, Master Doctor, now you have sent away my guests, I pray, who shall pay me for my a—

    [Faustus charms him dumb] Exeunt Hostess

DUCHESS   *[to the Duke]* My lord,

We are much beholding to this learned man.

DUKE   So are we, madam, which we will recompense

With all the love and kindness that we may.

His artful sport drives all sad thoughts away.

    Exeunt

买马——

　　　　[浮士德念咒,使马贩噤声]

罗宾　你记得我吗？你一天到晚只知道"天令令，地令令",还记得那狗——

　　　　[浮士德念咒,使马贩噤声。]众小丑下

女店主　谁来付酒账？博士大人,你听好了,你把我的顾客打发走,我要问问你,谁来付这份——

　　　　[浮士德念咒,使女店主噤声。]女店主下

公爵夫人　[对公爵]我的主人,这位博学的大师让我们大开眼界了。

公爵　是啊,夫人。我们应该报答他,

以我们所有的爱心与仁道：

他高超的魔法已使我们忧愁全消。

　　　　同下

ACT 5

第五幕

SCENE 1

Thunder and lightning. Enter Devils with covered dishes.
Mephistopheles leads them into Faustus' study. Then enter
Wagner

WAGNER   I think my master means to die shortly.

He has made his will and given all his wealth.

His house, his goods, and store of golden plate,

Besides two thousand ducats ready coined.

I wonder what he means. If death were nigh,

He would not frolic thus. He's now at supper

With the scholars, where there's such belly-cheer

As Wagner in his life ne'er saw the like.

And see where they come. Belike the feast is done.

Exit [Wagner.] Enter Faustus, Mephistopheles, and two or
three Scholars

FIRST SCHOLAR   Master Doctor Faustus, since our conference about fair
ladies—which was the beautifullest in all the world—we have
determined with ourselves that Helen of Greece was the admirablest
lady that ever lived. Therefore, Master Doctor, if you will do us so
much favour as to let us see that peerless dame of Greece, whom

第一场

　　雷电交加。若干魔鬼手托盖着的碟子上,在靡非斯特的率领下进入浮士德的书斋。瓦格纳然后上

瓦格纳　我觉得我的主人已来日无多,

　　他写下遗嘱,要将财富留给我:

　　除了现成的两千达克特[36]金银币,

　　还有房产、物器和镀金的餐具。

　　我不知道他此时是何样的心情。死亡临近,

　　他不该如此宽心;眼下他正跟几位学者

　　共进晚餐,餐桌上摆出的各种美味佳肴,

　　鄙人瓦格纳此生见所未见。

　　他们来了,想必宴席已结束。

　　　[瓦格纳]下。浮士德、靡非斯特,以及两三位学者上

学者甲　浮士德大师,关于世上美女的议题——谁乃世间最美——我们曾发表了各自的高见,并一致同意来自希腊的海伦超绝千古, 乃美中之魁。所以,浮士德大师,如果您肯施展大能,许我们一睹这位来自希腊, 为世人啧啧称赞的

189

all the world admires for majesty, we should think ourselves much

beholding unto you.

FAUSTUS   Gentlemen,

For that I know your friendship is unfeigned,

It is not Faustus' custom is to deny

The just request of those that wish him well:

You shall behold that peerless dame of Greece,

No otherwise for pomp or majesty

Than when Sir Paris crossed the seas with her

And brought the spoils to rich Dardania.

Be silent then, for danger is in words.

> *[Mephistopheles goes to the door.]   Music   sound   [s].*
> *Mephistopheles brings in Hellen. She passeth over the stage*

SECOND SCHOLAR   Was the fair Helen, whose admired worth

Made Greece with ten years' wars afflict poor Troy?

THIRD SCHOLAR   Too simple is my wit to tell her worth,

Whom all the world admires for majesty.

FIRST SCHOLAR   Now we have seen the pride of nature's works,

We'll take our leaves, and for this blessed sight

Happy and blest be Faustus evermore.

FAUSTUS   Gentlemen, farewell. The same I wish to you.

> *Exeunt Scholars. Enter an Old Man*

OLD MAN   O, gentle Faustus, leave the damned art,

This magic, that will charm thy soul to hell

And quite bereave thee of salvation!

绝代佳人的真实姿容，我等将对您佩服得五体
投地。

浮士德 先生们，

我知道你们的友谊真诚无虚；

对于良朋益友的正当要求，

小可浮士德没有拒绝之理。

你们将见到的这位希腊美人，

无论穿着打扮和美色姿容，

都与当年帕里斯漂洋过海，

带回特洛伊的那位一模一样。

大家别出声,不然有危险。

　　[靡非斯特走向门外。]乐声起。靡非斯特偕海伦

　　回。海伦款步走过舞台

学者乙 这就是导致希腊与可怜的特洛伊

发生十年战争的那位绝世美人?

学者丙 我才疏学浅,不知她美在哪里,

更不知世人为何将此女仰慕。

学者甲 我们已经见过自然的杰作,

就此辞别吧,为这次眼福,

但愿浮士德永远吉祥安康!

浮士德 再见,诸位先生。我也祝你们幸福长乐。

　　众学者下。一老者上

老者 亲爱的浮士德,丢掉该死的魔法吧,

它只会诱惑你的灵魂下地狱,

让你永远得不到上帝的救助!

Though thou hast now offended like a man,

Do not persever in it like a devil.

Though thou hast an amiable soul,

If sin by custom grow not into nature.

Then, Faustus, will repentance come too late;

Then thou art banished from the sight of heaven.

No mortal can express the pains of hell.

It may be this my exhortation

Seems harsh and all unpleasant. Let it not,

For, gentle son, I speak it not in wrath

Or envy of thee, but in tender love

And pity of thy future misery;

And so have hope that this my kind rebuke,

Checking the body, may amend thy soul.

FAUSTUS   Where art thou, Faustus? Wretch, what hast thou done?

Hell claims his rights, and with a roaring voice

Says, 'Faustus, come! Thine hour is almost come.'

Mephistopheles gives him a dagger

And Faustus now will come to do thee right.

[*Faustus prepares to stab himself*]

OLD MAN   O, stay, good Faustus, stay thy desperate steps!

I see an angel hovers o'er thy head,

And with a vial full of precious grace

Offers to pour the same into thy soul.

Then call for mercy, and avoid despair.

作为人类,你已犯下滔天大罪,

千万别像魔鬼那样执迷不悟。

只要罪恶尚未成为你的天性,

你依然,依然拥有可爱的魂灵。

浮士德啊,你迟迟不肯忏悔,

必将无缘享受天堂的美景。

人间凡人难描述地狱的痛苦。

也许我婆心苦口,你一概

视为空言虚语,但亲爱的人啊,

你可别这么想,要知道:

我说这话不为泄愤和妒忌,

全然为了爱你,担忧你的未来。

我希望:这番友爱的训诫,

能促你反省,从此悔过自新。

浮士德　你在哪里,浮士德?不幸的人啊,

你做了什么?拥有特权的地狱在高呼:

"浮士德,来吧,你的大限到了!"

靡非斯特递过一把匕首

浮士德,现在就主持正义吧。

[浮士德准备用匕首自杀]

老者　且慢,好浮士德,停止这疯狂的举动!

我看见一个天使飞翔在你头顶,

他手持一个装满神恩的瓶子,

随时准备将神恩洒向你的灵魂。

祈求怜悯吧,别走向万丈深渊。

FAUSTUS O friend, I feel thy words to comfort my distressed soul.

Leave me a while to ponder on my sins.

OLD MAN Faustus, I leave thee, but with grief of heart,

Fearing the enemy of thy hapless soul.

Exit [Old Man]

FAUSTUS Accursed Faustus, wretch, what hast thou done?

I do repent, and yet I do despair.

Hell strives with grace for conquest in my breast.

What shall I do to shun the snares of death?

MEPHISTOPHELES Thou traitor, Faustus, I arrest thy soul

For disobedience to my sovereign lord.

Revolt, or I'll in piecemeal tear thy flesh.

FAUSTUS I do repent I e'er offended him.

Sweet Mephistopheles, entreat thy lord

To pardon my unjust presumption,

And with my blood again I will confirm

The former vow I made to Lucifer.

MEPHISTOPHELES Do it then, Faustus, with unfeigned heart,

Lest greater danger do attend thy drift.

[Faustus cuts his arm and writes with his blood]

FAUSTUS Torment, sweet friend, that base and aged man

That durst dissuade me from thy Lucifer,

With greatest torments that our hell affords.

MEPHISTOPHELES His faith is great. I cannot touch his soul.

But what I may afflict his body with

浮士德　朋友,你的话安慰我痛苦的灵魂。

　　　　让我独自待一会,想想我的罪孽。

老者　浮士德,我离开你,心情好不沉重,

　　　　怕只怕敌人再来纠缠你不幸的灵魂。

　　　　　　[老者]下

浮士德　可怜而可恨的浮士德,你做了什么呀?

　　　　我要忏悔,但我的绝望依然。

　　　　地狱对抗神恩,压迫着我的心胸。

　　　　我如何才能摆脱死亡的罗网?

靡非斯特　逆贼浮士德,我要逮捕你,

　　　　因为你胆敢背弃我的君主。

　　　　回头吧,否则我要把你撕得粉碎!

浮士德　我悔恨我冒犯了地狱之主。

　　　　好靡非斯特,代我向冥帝求情,

　　　　宽恕我不该有的胡思乱想。

　　　　我要再次凭我的鲜血发誓:

　　　　我对魔王的誓约决不背弃!

靡非斯特　那就行动吧,浮士德,用你的真心,

　　　　否则你的前方就是更大的危险。

　　　　　　[浮士德割开手臂,蘸血书写]

浮士德　我的好友,你用地狱中最惨烈的

　　　　刑罚治一治那位下贱的老者,

　　　　是他大胆妄为,劝我背叛魔王。

靡非斯特　他信仰坚定,我伤不了他的灵魂。

　　　　但我可以试试,折磨一下他的肉体,

I will attempt, which is but little worth.

FAUSTUS   One thing, good servant, let me crave of thee,

To glut the longing of my heart's desire:

That I may have unto my paramour

That heavenly Helen, which I saw of late,

Whose sweet embraces may extinguish clear

Those thoughts that do dissuade me from my vow,

And keep my vow I made to Lucifer.

MEPHISTOPHELES   This, or what else my Faustus shalt desire,

Shall be performed in twinkling of an eye.

> *Enter Helen again [brought in by Mephistopheles], passing
> over between two Cupids*

FAUSTUS   Was this the face that launched a thousand ships

And burnt the topless towers of Ilium?

Sweet Helen, make me immortal with a kiss.

> *[They kiss]*

Her lips suck forth my soul. See where it flies!

Come, Helen, come, give me my soul again.

> *[They kiss again]*

Here will I dwell, for heaven is in these lips,

And all is dross that is not Helena.

I will be Paris, and for love of thee,

Instead of Troy shall Wittenberg be sacked,

And I will combat with weak Menelaus,

And wear thy colours on my plumed crest.

只怕这种折磨并无多大意义。

浮士德　我的好仆人,我还有一事相求,

请你务必满足这最大的愿望:

我想让绝代佳人海伦做我的情妇,

最近我见过她,她甜美的拥抱

定能将诱惑过我的种种杂念

一概消除,并促使我一心一意

去遵守我向魔王许下的誓约。

靡非斯特　举手之劳,顷刻之间就能做到,

浮士德想什么,就得到什么。

　　　海伦[在靡非斯特引领下]重上,从两位爱

　　神身边穿过

浮士德　就是这张脸调动了上千艘战船,

焚毁了高耸入云的特洛伊城堡?

亲爱的海伦,赐我永恒的一吻。

　　　[两人相吻]

她的红唇吸走了我的灵魂。看,它飞去了!

来,海伦,来,把灵魂还给我。

　　　[两人再吻]

我要留居于此,她的红唇就是天堂,

除了海伦,一切都是废物残渣。

我要成为帕里斯,为了你的爱,

让维腾堡代替特洛伊而毁灭,

我要与不中用的墨涅拉俄斯决斗,

盾牌的羽饰上挂出你的标识。

Yea, I will wound Achilles in the heel
And then return to Helen for a kiss.
O, thou art fairer than the evening's air,
Clad in the beauty of a thousand stars.
Brighter art thou than flaming Jupiter
When he appeared to hapless Semele,
More lovely than the monarch of the sky
In wanton Arethusa's azure arms;
And none but thou shalt be my paramour.

Exeunt

我还要刺伤阿喀琉斯的脚跟，
然后再回来与海伦深情亲吻。
啊，你的美胜过绚烂的晚霞，
无数的星星衬托出你的优雅。
当朱庇特在塞墨勒面前显形，[37]
他的光彩不如你浏亮晶莹；
即便他投入林中女神的酥胸，
这天界的君主也不如你可爱。
我的情人只有你，别人不配。

　　同下

SCENE 2

Thunder. Enter Lucifer, Beelzebub, and Mephistopheles [above]

LUCIFER   Thus from infernal Dis do we ascend

To view the subjects of our monarchy,

Those souls which sin seals the black sons of hell,

'Mong which as chief, Faustus, we come to thee,

Bringing with us lasting damnation

To wait upon thy soul. The time is come

Which makes it forfeit.

MEPHISTOPHELES   And this gloomy night

Here in this room will wretched Faustus be.

BEELZEBUB   And here we'll stay

To mark him how he doth demand himself.

MEPHISTOPHELES   How should he, but in desperate lunacy?

Fond worldling, now his heart-blood dries with grief;

His conscience kills it, and his labouring brain

Begets a world of idle fantasies

To overreach the devil. But all in vain.

His store of pleasures must be sauced with pain.

He and his servant Wagner are at hand,

200

第二场

雷声。魔王撒旦、别西卜、靡非斯特上

撒旦 我们从阴曹地府升起,来这里

造访受我们节制的人间苍生,

即那些罪恶昭彰的地狱子民;

他们当中为首的是浮士德博士,

我们来见他,带着万劫不复的

判决,准备取走他的灵魂。

时限已近,浮士德在劫难逃。

靡非斯特 今晚的天一片阴沉,浮士德

将在这个房间结束他的生命。

别西卜 我们在此等候,想看看

他今晚怎样将自己了断。

靡非斯特 他此刻思维混乱,神志癫狂,

伤心的凡夫,心中的血已干涸。

天良成凶手,劳碌的大脑滋生

一大堆古怪的思想,连魔鬼

也望尘莫及。但一切全是徒劳:

他的喜悦中必定掺和痛苦。

他刚才草拟了一份新的遗嘱,

Both come from drawing Faustus' latest will.

See where they come.

Enter Faustus and Wagner

FAUSTUS   Say, Wagner. Thou hast perused my will;

How dost thou like it?

WAGNER   Sir, so wondrous well

As in all humble duty I do yield

My life and lasting service for your love.

Enter the Scholars

FAUSTUS   Gramercies, Wagner.—Welcome, gentlemen.

[*Exit Wagner*]

FIRST SCHOLAR   Now, worthy Faustus, methinks your looks are changed.

FAUSTUS   O gentlemen!

SECOND SCHOLAR   What ails Faustus?

FAUSTUS   Ah, my sweet chamber-fellow! Had I lived with thee, then had I lived still, but now must die eternally. Look, sirs, comes he not? Comes he not?

FIRST SCHOLAR   O my dear Faustus, what imports this fear?

SECOND SCHOLAR   Is all our pleasure turned to melancholy?

THIRD SCHOLAR   [*to the other Scholars*] He is not well with being over-solitary.

SECOND SCHOLAR   If it be so, we'll have physicians, and Faustus shall be cured.

THIRD SCHOLAR   [*to Faustus*] 'Tis but a surfeit, sir. Fear nothing.

FAUSTUS   A surfeit of deadly sin, that hath damned both body and

他和助手瓦格纳就要过来了。

看，他们来了。

  浮士德、瓦格纳上

浮士德 瓦格纳，我的遗嘱你已看过；

你觉得怎样？

瓦格纳 先生，我觉得很好。

为了您的爱，我将竭诚为您效劳，

即便舍弃自己的性命也在所不惜。

  三学者上

浮士德 谢谢你，瓦格纳。——欢迎，诸位学友！

  [瓦格纳下]

学者甲 可敬的浮士德，您的气色不太好。

浮士德 唉！先生们哪。

学者乙 哪里不舒服吗？

浮士德 唉，我的同窗好友！如果我一直跟你们在一起，

我也许还好好地活着；但这回必死无疑了。看，先生，

他不是来了吗？他不是来了吗？

学者甲 我亲爱的浮士德，什么事让你这般恐惧？

学者乙 我们的欢乐都转化为忧伤了吗？

学者丙 [对其他学者]他的身体如此虚弱，想必是过于

孤独引起的。

学者乙 如果是这样，我们得去请医生，浮士德的病一定

能治好。

学者丙 [对浮士德]你仅仅是劳累过度，别担心。

浮士德 我这是作孽过度，如今灵魂和肉体都遭到报

soul.

SECOND SCHOLAR   Yet, Faustus, look up to heaven, and remember mercy is infinite.

FAUSTUS   But Faustus' offence can ne'er be pardoned. The serpent that tempted Eve may be saved, but not Faustus. O gentlemen, hear with patience, and tremble not at my speeches. Though my heart pant and quiver to remember that I have been a student here these thirty years. O, would I had never seen Wittenberg, never read book! And what wonders I have done, all Germany can witness, yea, all the world, for which Faustus hath lost both Germany and the world, yea, heaven itself—heaven, the seat of God, the throne of the blessed, the kingdom of joy—and must remain in hell for ever. Hell, O, hell, for ever! Sweet friends, what shall become of Faustus, being in hell for ever?

SECOND SCHOLAR   Yet, Faustus, call on God.

FAUSTUS   On God, whom Faustus hath abjured? On God, whom Faustus hath blasphemed? O my God, I would weep, but the devil draws in my tears. Gush forth blood instead of tears, yea, life and soul. O, he stays my tongue! I would lift up my hands, but see, they hold 'em, they hold 'em!

ALL   Who, Faustus?

FAUSTUS   Why, Lucifer and Mephistopheles. O gentlemen, I gave them my soul for my cunning.

ALL   O, God forbid!

FAUSTUS   God forbade it indeed, but Faustus hath done it. For the vain

204

应了。

学者乙　浮士德,那你就仰视天堂,然后想想无限的仁
慈吧。

浮士德　浮士德的罪过是无法被宽容了。即便引诱夏娃
的蛇能被拯救,浮士德也不能。诸位先生,耐心听我
说两句,不要这般紧张。一想起我曾经在这里治学三
十年,我的心就跳得厉害,就颤抖起来! 唉,如果我从
没来过维腾堡,从未读过书,那该多好。我曾经施行
过什么魔法,创造过怎样的奇迹,全德国、全世界可
见证;但为了这一切,浮士德已失去德国,失去世界,
对了,还失去天堂——天堂哪,那是上帝的居所,有
福者的家园,大欢喜的王国啊——浮士德只能永远待
在地狱里! 地狱,啊,万劫不复的地狱! 亲爱的朋友
们,浮士德永远沉沦在地狱,那将是怎样一番情景啊?

学者乙　浮士德,那你就向上帝求助吧。

浮士德　求助上帝?浮士德曾发誓背弃的那个上帝?曾亵
渎过的那个上帝? 我的上帝,我真想大声痛哭,但魔
鬼不许我哭。就让我的血喷涌吧,不是眼泪,是生命
和灵魂。哎哟,他不许我说话了!我想举起双手,但你
们看,他们把我的手按住了,他们把我的手按住了!

三学者　谁啊,浮士德?

浮士德　是魔王和靡非斯特。学友们哪,为了掌握魔法,
我已将自己的灵魂交给魔鬼了。

三学者　啊,这是上帝不允许的!

浮士德　上帝确实不允许,但浮士德偏偏做了。为了二十

pleasure of twenty-four years hath Faustus lost eternal joy and felicity. I writ them a bill with mine own blood. The date is expired. This is the time, and he will fetch me.

FIRST SCHOLAR   Why did not Faustus tell us of this before, that divines might have prayed for thee?

FAUSTUS   Oft have I thought to have done so, but the devil threatened to tear me in pieces if I named God, to fetch me body and soul if I once gave ear to divinity. And now 'tis too late. Gentlemen, away, lest you perish with me.

SECOND SCHOLAR   O, what shall we do to save Faustus?

FAUSTUS   Talk not of me, but save yourselves and depart.

THIRD SCHOLAR   God will strengthen me. I will stay with Faustus.

FIRST SCHOLAR   [*to the Third Scholar*] Tempt not God, sweet friend, but let us into the next room and pray for him.

FAUSTUS   Ay, pray for me, pray for me! And what noise soever you hear, come not unto me, for nothing can rescue me.

SECOND SCHOLAR   Pray thou, and we will pray that God may have mercy upon thee.

FAUSTUS   Gentlemen, farewell. If I live till morning,
I'll visit you; if not, Faustus is gone to hell.

ALL   Faustus, farewell.

Exeunt Scholars

MEPHISTOPHELES   Ay, Faustus, now thou hast no hope of heaven;
Therefore despair. Think only upon hell,
For that must be thy mansion, there to dwell.

四年无聊的欢乐，浮士德已经失去永恒的欢乐和幸
福。我用我的血写过一份契约，它的期限到了。大限
就在眼前，过一会他就要来带走我。

学者甲　你为什么不早告诉我们这件事呢？牧师可以为
你祈祷啊。

浮士德　我也早想过这样做，但魔鬼威胁说：如果我提
起上帝，他就把我撕成碎片；如果我去找牧师忏
悔，他就掳走我的肉体和灵魂。如今这一切都太
迟了。学友们，你们走吧，别受我的连累了。

学者乙　啊，我们如何才能拯救浮士德呢？

浮士德　别再谈论我了，还是拯救你们自己，赶快离开吧。

学者丙　上帝给我力量。我要与浮士德在一起。

学者甲　[对学者丙]别试探上帝，我的好友，我们还是到
隔壁房间为他祈祷吧。

浮士德　好，为我祈祷，为我祈祷! 你们听得到的，我都听
不到，任何人都救不了我。

学者乙　祈祷吧，浮士德。我们会为你祈祷，祈祷上帝怜
悯你。

浮士德　再见吧，学友们。如能活到天明，我会去找你们的；
如果没有去，那浮士德就已经下地狱了。

三学者　再见，浮士德。

　　　　　三学者下

靡非斯特　浮士德，你没有希望进天堂，
别妄想! 一心想想地狱吧，
那里才是你的居所，你的归宿。

FAUSTUS   O thou bewitching fiend, 'twas thy temptation

Hath robbed me of eternal happiness.

MEPHISTOPHELES   I do confess it, Faustus, and rejoice.

'Twas I that, when thou wert i'the way to heaven,

Dammed up thy passage. When thou took'st the book

To view the Scriptures, then I turned the leaves

And led thine eye.

What, weep'st thou?   'Tis too late. Despair, farewell!

Fools that will laugh on earth must weep in hell.

Exit [Mephistopheles]. Enter the Good Angel and the Bad

Angel at several doors

GOOD ANGEL   O Faustus, if thou hadst given ear to me,

Innumberable joys had followed thee.

But thou didst love the world.

BAD ANGEL   Gave ear to me,

And now must taste hell's pains perpetually.

GOOD ANGEL   O, what will all thy riches, pleasures, pomps

Avail thee now?

BAD ANGEL   Nothing but vex thee more,

To want in hell, that had on earth such store.

Music while the throne descends

GOOD ANGEL   O, thou hast lost celestial happiness,

Pleasures unspeakable, bliss without end.

Hadst thou affected sweet divinity,

Hell or the devil had had no power on thee.

浮士德 你这蛊惑人心的魔鬼,正是你的引诱

导致我丧失永恒的天堂之福。

靡非斯特 这我承认,浮士德,我为此而欣喜。

当你行走在天堂的路上,正是我

堵住你的去路。当你拿起《圣经》

准备阅读,也是我引诱你丢下它,

转而着迷于魔法。怎么,你哭了?

太迟了!绝望去吧,再见,浮士德!

在人间欢笑的傻瓜,在地狱必然痛哭。

　　　[靡非斯特]下。好天使、坏天使各

　　　自上

好天使 浮士德啊,如果你听从我的忠言,

无穷尽的欢乐将与你形影相随。

但你偏只爱碌碌凡尘。

坏天使 如今你听从我,

地狱的痛苦伴随着你,直到永远。

好天使 你的财富、欢乐和声誉,

如今于你又有何益?

坏天使 无益,徒增你的烦恼,

人间的富埒王侯,在地狱一无所有。

　　　乐声起,神龛下降

好天使 你已经失去天堂的幸福,

那无法用语言描述的大欢喜。

如果你一直挚爱神圣的天国,

地狱和魔鬼就接近不了你。

Hadst thou kept on that way, Faustus, behold

In what resplendent glory thou hadst set

In yonder throne, like those bright shining saints,

And triumphed over hell. That hast thou lost.

And now, poor soul, must thy good angel leave thee.

The jaws of hell are open to receive thee.

[The throne ascends.] Exit [Good Angel]. Hell is discovered

BAD ANGEL   Now Faustus, let thine eyes with horror stare

Into that vast perpetual torture-house.

There are the Furies tossing damned souls

On burning forks; their bodies boil in lead.

There are live quarters broiling on the coals,

That ne'er can die. This ever-burning chair

Is for o'er-tortured souls to rest them in.

These that are fed with sops of flaming fire

Were gluttons, and loved only delicates,

And laughed to see the poor starve at their gates.

But yet all these are nothing. Thou shalt see

Ten thousand tortures that more horrid be.

FAUSTUS   O, I have seen enough to torture me!

BAD ANGEL   Nat, thou must feel them, taste the smart of all.

He that loves the pleasure must for pleasure fall.

And so leave thee, Faustus, till anon;

Then wilt thou tumble in confusion.

Exit [Bad Angel]. The clock strikes eleven

如果你一直走在正道上，

如今一定端坐在神龛，

享受战胜地狱的荣光，

一如金光闪耀的圣徒。但如今，

可悲的灵魂，你的好天使只能离你而去，

只有地狱张开大口接纳你。

　　　　[神龛升起,好天使]下。地狱显现

坏天使　浮士德,睁开你恐惧的双眼

看看这地老天荒的行刑室。

复仇神挥舞火红的钢叉,折磨着

有罪的灵魂;他们就在铅水中挣扎;

活生生的肢体在永不熄灭的

炭火上炙烤。这座椅也在不停燃烧,

受过酷刑后的灵魂就安顿在这里。

这些被火焰吞没的人都是贪食者,

他们最爱美味佳肴,喜欢嘲笑

家门口出现的饥肠辘辘的穷人。

但这都算不了什么,过一会

你还将看到比这更可怖的诸多景象。

浮士德　啊,这一切已足够让我心惊。

坏天使　你得先感受一下,尝尝其中滋味。

贪图享乐的人,得因享乐而沉沦。

我要走了,浮士德,下次再见:

我等待你最后的毁灭。

　　　　[坏天使]下。时钟敲响十一点

211

FAUSTUS   O Faustus,

      Now has thou but one bare hour to live,

      And then thou must be damned perpetually.

      Stand still, you ever-moving spheres of heaven,

      That time may cease, and midnight never come!

      Fair nature's eye, rise, rise again, and make

      Perpetual day; or let this hour be but

      A year, a month, a week, a natural day,

      That Faustus may repent and save his soul!

      O lente, lente currite noctis equi!

      The stars move still; time runs, the clock will strike;

      The devil will come, and Faustus must be damned.

      O, I'll leap up to heaven! Who pulls me down?

      One drop of blood would save me. O, my Christ!

      Rend not my heart for naming of my Christ!

      Yet will I call on him. O, spare me, Lucifer!

      Where is it now? 'Tis gone;

      And see a theat'ning arm, an angry brow.

      Mountains and hills, come, come, and fall on me,

      And hide me from the heavy wrath of heaven!

      No? Then will I headlong run into the earth.

      Gape, earth! O, no, it will not harbour me.

      You stars that reigned at my nativity,

      Whose influence hath allotted death and hell,

      Now draw up Faustus like a foggy mist.

浮士德　浮士德啊，

你的生命还有一小时，

然后你就必遭天谴，万劫不复。

不断运行的天体啊，停一停吧，

好让时光凝固，子夜永不降临!

自然的明眸啊，升起吧，快快升起，

养育出恒久的白天，把这一钟点

化为一年，一月，一周，或一整天，

好让浮士德有缘忏悔，拯救灵魂!

哟，慢点，慢点，黑夜的骏马![38]

但星星、时光没有停步，时钟就要敲响，

魔鬼就要到来，浮士德难逃天罚。

哟，我要纵身跃向天堂! 谁在拽我?

我的基督啊，你的一滴血就能救我!

我呼喊了基督，别因此撕碎我的心!

我还得央求他:魔王啊，放过我吧!

上帝在哪里啊? 他不在这里了;

眼前只有愤怒的臂膀和皱起的眉头。

山岳啊，来吧，来吧，把我压住，

好让我隐身躲避上天的雷霆之怒。

躲不掉吗? 那就只好摔落尘土了。

大地啊，张嘴吧! 怎么，大地不容我?

那掌管人类生辰的星星又在哪里?

你们的运行决定我的寿限和天谴，

请你们将我吸上天，如一缕雾气，

Into the entrails of yon labouring cloud,

That when you vomit forth into the air,

My limbs may issue from your smoky mouths,

But let my soul mount and ascend to heaven.

The watch strikes

O, half the hour is past! 'Twill all be past anon.

O, if the soul must suffer for my sin,

Impose some end to my incessant pain.

Let Faustus live in hell a thousand years,

A hundred thousand, and at last be saved.

No end is limited to damned souls.

Why wert thou not a creature wanting soul?

Or why is this immortal that thou hast?

O, Pythagoras' *metempsychosis*, were that true,

This soul should fly from me and I be changed

Into some brutish beast.

All beasts are happy, for, when they die,

Their souls are soon dissolved in elements;

But mine must live still to be plagued in hell.

Curst be the parents that engendered me!

No, Faustus, curse thyself. Curse Lucifer,

That hath deprived thee of the joys of heaven.

The clock strikes twelve

It strikes, it strikes! Now, body, turn to air,

Or Lucifer will bear thee quick to hell.

允许我进入那奔腾不息的云层，
这样，当你们向着太空喷吐烟霞，
我的肢体就能从你们的大嘴抖落，
我的灵魂就能升起，进入天堂。

　　钟声又起

啊，又过半小时！大限很快到了。
如果我的灵魂一定得因罪而受罚，
就给我的痛苦设定一个终期吧。
让浮士德在地狱待上一千年，
十万年也行，只要最终能得救。
但对遭天谴的灵魂，没有终期可言。
你为何不去做一个没有灵魂的生物？
为何偏要做一个有灵魂的凡夫俗子？
如果真有毕达哥拉斯所说的轮回，
我的灵魂脱离肉体后，我也许
可转世为一头生性残暴的野兽。
所有的野兽都快乐：它们死时，
它们的灵魂很快化解为基本元素；
但我的灵魂却始终得在地狱受苦。
生我养我的父母啊，我诅咒你们！
喔，不，浮士德，你该诅咒自己！诅咒撒旦！
正是他剥夺了你来自天堂的欢乐。

　　时钟敲响十二点

到点了，到点了！让肉体化为
空气，让撒旦将你押进地狱吧。

O soul, be changed into small waterdrops,
And fall into the ocean, ne'er be found!

Thunder, and enter the Devils

O, mercy, heaven, look not so fierce on me!
Adders and serpents, let me breathe a while!
Ugly hell, gape not! Come not, Lucifer!
I'll burn my books. O, Mephistopheles!

Exeunt

灵魂啊,你就化为小小的水滴,

汇入大海大洋,从此永远消失吧!

    雷声。众魔上

苍天啊,怜悯我,别让我太痛苦!

毒蛇们,你们允许我喘口气!

丑陋的地狱,别张口! 魔王,别过来!

我要烧掉我的书。该死的靡非斯特哟!

    同下

SCENE 3

Enter the Scholars

FIRST SCHOLAR   Come gentlemen, let us go visit Faustus,

For such a dreadful night was never seen

Since first the world's creation did begin.

Such fearful shrieks and cries were never heard.

Pray heaven the doctor have escaped the danger.

SECOND SCHOLAR   Oh, help us, heaven! See, here are Faustus' limbs,

And torn asunder bu the hand of death.

THIRD SCHOLAR   The devils whom Faustus served have torn him thus.

For, 'twixt the hours of twelve and one, methought

I heard him shriek and call aloud for help,

At which self time the house seemed all on fire

With dreadful horror of these damned fiends.

SECOND SCHOLAR   Well, gentlemen, though Faustus' end be such

As every Christian heart laments to think on,

Yet, for he was a scholar, once admired

For wondrous knowledge in our German schools,

We'll give his mangled limbs due burial;

And all the students, clothed in mourning black,

第三场

三学者上

学者甲　来吧,学友们,去看看浮士德。

从世界被创造的第一天算起,

如此可怕的夜晚见所未见,

如此凄凉的尖叫闻所未闻。

愿上天保佑我们的博士逢凶化吉。

学者乙　我的老天爷! 看,这是浮士德的肢体,

死神的毒手已经将他分尸了。

学者丙　定是浮士德召唤过的魔鬼肢解了他,

昨天晚上十二点至一点之间,

我曾听见他的尖叫和呼救声。

该死的魔鬼制造骇人的恐怖,

那场景就像整幢楼房着了火。

学者乙　诸位学友,浮士德死亡的惨状

每个基督徒都不忍心再看。

他毕竟是个学者,渊博的学识

曾为德国所有的学校所钦佩。

把他的残肢凑起来掩埋了吧。

所有的学生都穿上黑色的丧服,

Shall wait upon his heavy funeral.

Exeunt

为浮士德举行隆重的葬礼。

　　同下

EPILOGUE

Enter Chorus

CHORUS   Cut is the branch that might have grown full straight,

And burned is Apollo's laurel bough,

That sometime grew within this learned man.

Faustus is gone. Regard his hellish fall,

Whose fiendful fortune may exhort the wise,

Only to wonder at unlawful things,

Whose deepness doth entice such forward wits

To practice more than heavenly power permits.

    [Exit]

Terminat hora diem; terminat auctor opus.

收场白

解说员上
可能长成大树的枝条就此折断，
阿波罗植在博学者心胸的桂枝，
也已被焚，化成了一堆灰烬。
浮士德走了，想想他悲惨的下场吧。
他遭受的厄运足以告诫贤明之士：
无法无天的游戏只可一喷了之，
因为个中奥妙容易误导人间英杰，
让他们做出为上天不容的蠢事。
　　［下］

一天告罄，全剧告终。

COMMENTS/注释

[1] 特拉西梅诺,在意大利境内。公元前217年,汉尼拔率迦太基军队在此打败古罗马人。

[2] 玛尔斯,古罗马神话中的战神。

[3] 指诗人。

[4] 上行是拉丁文引文,下行是浮士德的英文翻译。下文中的引文也有许多类似情况。

[5] 盖仑(129—199),古罗马著名医师、自然科学家和哲学家。

[6]《民法大全》,东罗马帝国皇帝查士丁尼一世(约483—565)主持编纂的一部汇编式法典,是罗马法的集大成者。

[7] 参见《新约·罗马书》第6章第23节。

[8] 参见《新约·约翰一书》第1章第8节。

[9] 浮士德计划废除学校所推行的节俭制度。

[10] 帕马,西班牙王子,1579—1592年间出任荷兰总督。

[11] 1585年,帕马公爵围攻安特卫普,守兵用装满火药的船炸毁安特卫普大桥。

[12] 穆赛俄斯,古希腊神话中的歌手、预言家,俄耳甫斯的得意弟子(一说是儿子)。

[13] 阿格里巴,当时民间著名的魔术师。

[14] 培根(1561—1626),英国思想家,实验科学的先驱。阿尔伯特

(约1200—1280),中世纪欧洲的重要哲学家、神学家。

[15] 瓦格纳玩文字游戏,意思是说,"天知道"不可以推理为"我不知道"。

[16] "早晨之子"是堕落之前的撒旦的称呼。

[17] 虱草的种子可用来制作驱虫剂。

[18] 埃姆登,德国北部一港口城市,以商业繁华著称。

[19] 参见《新约·提摩太前书》第6章第11节。

[20] 珀涅罗珀,荷马史诗《奥德赛》中俄底修斯的妻子,以忠贞、贤惠著称。

[21] 示巴女王,参见《旧约·列王记上》第10章第1节。

[22] 指马店的老板。

[23] 意谓给丈夫戴绿帽子。旧时,在西方,人们认为妻子有外遇,丈夫头上会长出角。

[24] 俄诺涅,荷马史诗《伊利亚特》中帕里斯的前妻。帕里斯在战场上中了毒箭,俄诺涅拒绝救治,帕里斯毒发身死。俄诺涅后因悔恨自杀。

[25] 特里尔,德国西部一城市。浮士德与靡非斯特的旅行从特里尔到巴黎,然后向东抵达曼恩河与莱茵河的交汇处,再往南到达意大利。

[26] 坎帕尼亚,意大利南部一省,那不勒斯即在该省境内。

[27] 马罗(前70—前19),即古罗马诗人维吉尔,《埃涅阿斯记》的作者,全名是普伯琉斯·维吉琉斯·马罗。据传,诗人曾利用魔法在岩壁中凿出一条通道。他的陵墓在那不勒斯。

[28] 德意志国王腓特烈一世(约1122—1190)曾宣布自己在意大利拥有无限的权力。他也曾扶立伪教皇维克多四世。1176年,他的

军队为伦巴第联盟军所败,次年向教皇亚历山大三世悔罪。此
　　处马洛的描写有杜撰的成分。

[29] 西吉斯孟,神圣罗马帝国皇帝(1411—1437;1433年加冕)。教皇
朱利斯三世是16世纪人。此处马洛的描写完全是虚构的。

[30] 亚克托安,古希腊神话中的猎人。因偷看女神狄安娜沐浴,女神
　　把他变成一头鹿,结果他被自己的猎狗咬死。

[31] 大流士三世(? —前330),波斯国王,公元前333年被亚历山大
　　打败。

[32] 班佛里奥在窗口时,显然已经受到魔鬼的攻击。

[33] 法新,英国1961年前流通的铜币,等于四分之一便士。

[34] 罗宾处在酒醉状态,当自己仍在酒店中。显然,这班酒徒是着了
　　浮士德的魔法才过来供公爵消遣的。

[35] 马车夫想以此验证一下浮士德是否装了假腿。

[36] 达克特,中世纪许多欧洲国家通用的金币或银币的名称。

[37] 塞墨勒,古希腊神话中宙斯的情人,要求宙斯以神的全部雄伟
　　姿态出现,结果被电火烧成灰烬。此处朱庇特即宙斯。

[38] 古罗马诗人奥维德(前43—17/18)的诗句,原文为拉丁文。